P9-CMW-782

KIKI
KALLIRA
CONQUERS A CURSE

ALSO BY SANGU MANDANNA

Kiki Kallira Breaks a Kingdom

KIKI KALLIRA

CONQUERS A CURSE

Sangu Mandanna

VIKING

VIKING
An imprint of Penguin Random House LLC, New York

First published in the United States of America by Viking,
an imprint of Penguin Random House LLC, 2022

Visit us online at penguinrandomhouse.com.

Library of Congress Cataloging-in-Publication Data is available.

Book manufactured in Canada

ISBN 9780593207000

10 9 8 7 6 5 4 3 2 1

FRI

Design by Kate Renner
Text set in Casus Pro

To Penny, who makes these stories possible.

KIKI KALLIRA
CONQUERS A CURSE

1

"Kiki, why is there a crow on my kitchen table?"

I glared at the crow in question, but he just shrugged his wings unrepentantly.

It was a *little* unfair that my mother saw a crow in our kitchen and immediately assumed it had something to do with me. On the other hand, she wasn't exactly wrong, so my indignation was probably misplaced.

Both Mum and the crow were staring expectantly at me, but my mind was a little busy Overthinking.

When that happens, my thoughts go something like this: *if I tell Mum the truth she might not believe me or she'll think I'm hallucinating, but if I lie to her I'll be stuck lying to her forever and I don't want to do that, but if I tell her the truth she might not believe me or she'll think—*

"Kiki," Mum said in a voice that would have made demon kings quake. We could have really used her when Mahishasura, the demon king, was terrorizing my imaginary kingdom a few months ago.

"He's my friend," I blurted out.

Mum blinked. "The crow? Are you telling me you found him, fed him, and now he hangs around all the time hoping for more? If that's the case, Kiki, I really don't see why he has to be *indoors*. What if he's covered in fleas? Do birds get fleas?"

"Oh, we don't have to worry about that," I said at once, before I could stop myself. "He's magical. He doesn't get parasites or diseases or anything."

Mum stared at me in stunned silence. I winced. Across the kitchen, the crow smacked a wing over his eyes.

"Magical," said Mum. She looked uncertain, like she wasn't sure whether to play along as she used to when I was six or call my doctor and ask if the medication she'd prescribed had any peculiar side effects we should know about.

It had been a long day. I'd had school and Mum had

been working, and then we'd had to go straight to the doctor for my monthly "How are things going?" appointment, then to the supermarket, then to the food bank to drop off what we'd bought, and then, finally, back home. So we were both tired, and Pip could *really* have chosen his timing better, but it was too late to just breeze past it now.

It was time to tell Mum everything.

"Okay," I said, collapsing into one of the chairs at the table. I pointed at the crow. "This is Pip."

"Isn't that what you named your imaginary friend when you were little?" Mum asked, eyeing Pip like she wasn't entirely comfortable with me sitting so close to him.

I nodded. "This is him."

"You mean you've named the crow Pip, too?"

"No, I mean this is *that* Pip. My Pip."

Mum stared at me. I stared back. She sighed. "Kiki, I would really prefer not to adopt a crow as a pet, but I'm willing to consider it if you're really attached to him. You don't have to make things up."

"But I'm not," I said, wondering if it was going to be possible to convince her. "Mum, I promise. I'm not making this up, and it's not the mela-thingy that Dr. Muzembe gave me to help me sleep, either."

"Melatonin," she corrected me automatically.

I looked at Pip. His black crow eyes twinkled at me, full of mischief. "You could at least wave or something," I said to him, exasperated. "You're the one who came out here instead of hiding in my room like we agreed. The least you can do is help me prove you're not a normal crow!"

With an obliging ruffle of his feathers, Pip raised one wing and waved at Mum.

Mum blinked. "Did he just—"

Perking up, because this was maybe my best way to make Mum believe the impossible, I said, "Pip, hop from one foot to the other."

Pip hopped from one foot to the other. Mum's eyes widened.

"Do that thing you did on my birthday last month."

Pip opened his beak and, puffing his chest out, started to make the most horrible cawing noises. Somewhere in the cacophony, though, was the unmistakable tune of the "Happy Birthday" song.

By this point, Mum's eyes were practically popping

right out of her head. She stared at Pip for a full minute before turning back to me. "Okay," she said in the voice of someone who has just been clonked on the head. "Explain."

"You have to promise to stay calm."

"I think that's a bit much to ask, don't you?"

"Fair enough." I bit my lip. Pip hopped onto my shoulder. "So the thing is . . ."

Back in October, the morning after I came out of my sketchbook world and back into the *real* world, I'd told Mum the truth about my worrying. I had told her how bad it had gotten, how I couldn't sleep because my brain was so noisy, how ugly and frightening and persistent some of my thoughts were—all of it. When I was done, I'd asked for help, and Mum had given it to me. She'd taken me to our doctor, who had put me on a waiting list for children's mental health services. While we waited, Dr. Muzembe had prescribed me melatonin to help me sleep and had suggested a few techniques I could try when things got bad.

Since then, the anxiousness and obsessive thoughts hadn't gone away, and I had been told repeatedly that they probably never would, but I felt like they were easier to cope with. Weirdly enough, just being able to talk about how I was feeling, without feeling ashamed or guilty like I used to, had made me feel a whole lot better. The melatonin helped me sleep at night. And Mum was always there for me.

But I'd never told her about the sketchbook, my made-up kingdom, or Mahishasura. It had been *awful* keeping such an exciting secret to myself, but what else could I have done? Sprung it on her over dinner one evening? *Mother, I created a magical kingdom in my sketchbook, and a demon king from Indian folklore brought it to life, so then I had to travel into my sketchbook kingdom to stop him and save everyone, which I did by using my really cool pencil magic and trapping the demon king in a collapsing palace. This pasta is really yummy, by the way.*

Yeah, I wouldn't have believed me, either.

But now that Pip had taken matters into his own wings, and had also given me the closest thing to proof I could offer, I could tell her.

So I did.

By the time I was done, Mum had the oddest look on

her face. She had looked bemused, appalled, and entertained at different points of my tale, almost like she'd let herself get swept up in what sounded like an awfully fun story, but *this* expression was something else. I couldn't find a name for it.

"Mum?" I prompted, when she didn't say anything. "Are you okay?"

A tiny smile lifted the corners of her mouth. "It's a funny thing. You know I illustrate and animate other people's stories for work, but there was a time when I used to make up the stories, too. Around the time you were born, *I* had a sketchbook with my own made-up world."

"Really?"

"It wasn't much like yours, by the sounds of it," she said. "Your dad loved it. I think that's why I stopped after he, well, you know. After." *After he died*, she meant. Clearing her throat, Mum went on, in a different tone of voice, "And of course, *my* world wasn't real."

I grimaced. "You don't believe me."

"It's not that I don't believe you," she said. "I mean, considering *that*"—she gestured somewhat helplessly to Pip—"it's hard not to believe you. But it's also hard to accept that everything you just told me could have actually happened. You're asking me to believe that while I was asleep in my bed, you, my only child and the most important thing in the world to me, were in an entirely different universe, in grave danger, and I might never have seen you again."

I felt my cheeks heat with guilt. Mum had already lost my dad, and now I was telling her that she'd come really close to losing me, too. Maybe this was why the kids in stories never told their parents what they were up to (assuming they *had* parents, or parents they actually liked, which was by no means a given). As someone who was a little too familiar with what it felt like to worry about the people I loved, I felt terrible for making my mother worry about me.

"But it's over now," I said. "I'm safe. And the gateway between the two worlds is sealed, so I can never go back."

"You don't sound happy about that," she said shrewdly.

I shrugged.

Mum looked at Pip, who had his beak in an open bag of donuts on the counter, and then back at me. "And you're saying all this *really* happened?"

I could tell she still didn't totally believe me. To be fair, it was a lot to ask of someone.

"You can look through my sketchbook if you like?" I offered.

"I'd love to," she said. She kept blinking, like she was quite sure she was going to wake up from a dream at any moment. Considering I'd fainted—actually, literally *fainted*—when I first arrived in my made-up universe, I thought she was handling it pretty well. "Why don't I put a pizza in the oven while you fetch it?"

Once dinner was ready, we sat back down at the table and she leafed through my sunshine-yellow sketchbook, forgetting entirely about her half of the pizza. She didn't even notice that Pip kept edging closer and closer to it.

"These are beautiful, Kiki," Mum said, gently running her fingers over one of my early sketches of Ashwini. "There are some things I can teach you, to improve your technique with poses and shading, but no one can teach heart. And your art has *so* much heart."

I blushed, my mouth too full of pizza to reply. Mum fell silent again as she reached the last fifth or so of the sketchbook, where my actual art stopped and the final pages became a re-creation of my time in the other world. Here, the drawings looked like an animated movie, the colors vivid and almost unreal, the pages almost breathing. Her eyes grew wide, like she could feel the magic that still lingered in the book.

"I think I'm going to need to sleep on this," she said at last. "This is a *lot*."

"Okay," I said. "We can talk about this whenever you want."

But before she handed back the sketchbook, she said, her eyes searching mine, "*This* is what got you through all those months, isn't it? Before I realized how bad things were?"

I hated that she blamed herself for not seeing how hideous I'd been feeling. How could she have seen it when I had made a choice to hide it? But I knew better than to argue with her. ("I'm your mother," she'd said the last time I'd tried. "I *should* have seen it.")

So I just nodded. "That sketchbook saved me."

"Okay," she said, and kissed me on the top of my head.

I helped her with the dishes, took my melatonin, and went to bed. And slept.

It was so *nice* to be able to sleep!

The next morning, Pip was in a weird mood. As I got dressed for school, I noticed him pecking repeatedly at my sketchbook. *The* sketchbook, as opposed to the new unmagical sketchbook I'd been doodling in for the past couple of months.

"What are you doing?" I demanded. "Do you want me to open it?"

He gave a caw that sounded like *yes*.

I huffed and opened the sketchbook, flipping through it until Pip nipped at my hand to stop me. I flicked him irritably on the beak as I withdrew my hand. He'd made me stop at a fully inked, colored drawing of Lej, who was scowling at something or the other. Probably me. It was one of the pages from the "when Kiki was in Mysore" section of the book.

Pip put one foot over the page to make sure it stayed open and fluffed his wings in satisfaction.

"That's what you wanted?" I asked. "You wanted to look at *Lej*, of all people?"

But as soon as I said it, I knew it was a silly thing to say. Lej and I hadn't exactly been the best of friends, but Pip had grown up with him and had loved him. Maybe he just wanted to see his face again. He'd chosen to leave the Kiki universe at the same time I did so that he could stay with me, and I knew he missed his family.

"Okay," I said more gently, picking up my satchel. "I'll leave it open for you."

But when I got back from school that afternoon, Pip wasn't the only Crow in my bedroom.

Lej was there, too.

2

"Gah!" I spluttered.

Of course, if there were ever a time to garble out unintelligible nonsense, this would surely be it. After all, hadn't I been told almost three months ago that the tear between the two universes would close forever? Hadn't I accepted that I might never find a way back to my made-up kingdom? (Or queendom? It *did* have a queen now, after all.)

But here, somehow, was Lej, standing in my bedroom. In my house. In London. In the real world.

"Gah?" he repeated, raising his eyebrows. That expression of maddening superiority was just as I remembered it.

Like most of the people I had met in the Kiki universe,

Lej's accent was just a more proper version of mine. My brain had, for reasons of its own, imagined everyone speaking like characters in an epic fantasy. Or like my mother, really, whose crisply formed syllables definitely resembled those of an elf in *The Lord of the Rings*. Only in *her* case, it was because she'd grown up in India, where she'd learned English from her parents, who had, in turn, learned it at school from elderly British nuns. I wasn't entirely sure why elderly British nuns and fantasy elves sounded so alike, but who was I to quibble with it?

Either way, I wished Lej didn't have that particular accent. It lent itself a little too well to haughty superiority.

As if he needed any help.

So I looked down my nose at him, which is an extremely difficult thing to do to someone who is taller than you, and said, "Your hair's grown a bit."

He made a sound that could have been a laugh. "Hello to you, too."

"How are you here?" I asked incredulously. I glanced behind him, at my sketchbook, which was still lying open to the painting of his face. "Is the tear open again?"

"*A* tear is open, but it's not the old tear," he said. He

turned away from me and went to the window. "Wow. Is it always so busy out there?"

Traffic wasn't really a thing in the other world, so I could understand his amazement.

"You haven't seen anything until you've seen rush hour," I said, waving a hand dismissively. "How did the tear open?"

"Chamundeshwari got the Good Witch to do it," he said.

"I didn't know the Good Witch could do that!"

"Neither did we, until she did it."

To be fair, that did sound like the Good Witch in a nutshell. She was certainly a witch, but the *good* part was still somewhat in question. We'd rescued her from Mahishasura's prison, and she'd helped us in return, but getting her to tell us anything useful had been like getting blood out of a stone.

My eyes fell on Pip, who was perched on my bookshelf pecking at the crumbs of a cookie he must have swiped during the day, and suddenly a whole lot of things made sense. "You knew!" I said. "I don't know how, but you knew!"

His beak couldn't grin, but his eyes twinkled.

"That's why you showed up in the kitchen yesterday and forced me to tell Mum about you. You knew I'd get the sketchbook out of my secret drawer to show it to her." I pinched the bridge of my nose, trying to maintain some control over the way my thoughts were running to and fro. "That's why you wanted me to open the book to that painting of Lej, wasn't it? You knew that was where the tear had opened."

Pip preened, obviously pleased with himself.

I spared him a scowl before turning back to Lej. "So are you here just because you missed me?"

"I missed you the way one misses an outbreak of lice," Lej said in what was, for him, a pretty affectionate tone.

"It brings me such joy to know some things will always stay the same," I replied. "Your lack of charm, for one thing."

He snorted, like he'd been surprised into laughter and had tried to hold it back. "I'm not here because I wanted to experience rush hour in London, Kiki," he admitted. "I'm here because Mysore is in trouble."

"Again?" I asked in disbelief.

"And we need you," he said. "Again."

I couldn't resist. "That must have been hard for you to say."

He crossed his arms over his chest and glared.

"Do *not* let my mother find out that you need my help," I said. "When I told her about the Kikiverse and all the Mahishasura stuff last night, she didn't do so well with the idea that she almost lost me and didn't even know it."

"What," Lej said very slowly, "did you just call it?"

"Call what?"

"The other world."

I frowned, mentally replayed what I'd said, and felt my cheeks go red. *Crimson.* "Nothing."

"You called it the Kikiverse."

"I did not!"

"You absolutely did." Lej was grinning now. Even Pip, the turncoat, was flat on his back on the bookshelf, screeching with what I could only assume was laughter. "You called it the Kikiverse! You know it, I know it, and Pip knows it."

I stayed silent, my cheeks still uncomfortably hot.

"I've missed your ego," Lej said fondly. "It was always so entertaining."

"Oh, shut up," I growled. "And I meant what I said about Mum. She'll absolutely murder you if she thinks you're going to drag me off into mortal peril again. Which," I added, perking up at happy visions of Mum ridding two universes of Lej, "might not be the worst thing in the world."

"I've faced scarier things than your mother," said Lej, rolling his eyes.

"I really don't think you have."

It was at this precise moment that two things happened simultaneously. One: I remembered that today was Tuesday, and that meant that, like every other Tuesday since her baby brother had been born, Emily would be staying over to give her mum a break from having three kids in the house. And two: we all heard Mum's voice, right outside my bedroom door, saying, "Kiki, Emily's here! Do you two want—"

Mum didn't finish her sentence because that was the point at which she opened the door and saw Pip, Lej, and me.

She blinked. Emily, standing beside her, blinked.

"Um, this is Lej," I said.

Mum and Emily looked at Lej. Then they looked at the painting of his face in my sketchbook, lying open on the desk right beside him. Then they looked back at him.

Emily, of course, then looked at me with sympathy. "Well, that's mortifying," she said.

"Oh, for heaven's sake," I huffed, slamming the sketchbook closed. "I haven't been sitting here painting portraits of his face—"

"No one is more relieved than I," said Lej.

I ignored him. "He came *out* of that portrait. I invented him."

"Only in the loosest possible sense," Lej assured everyone.

Mum said, "Oh my god, it's all true," and sat down on my bed so fast I was pretty sure her legs had refused to hold her up anymore.

And Emily said, "None of this makes sense to me," but she sounded like she was rather enjoying herself.

At that point, there was nothing to be done except tell Emily everything. It was a little trickier than telling Mum had been, not least because Lej felt the need to constantly interrupt me to share his unflattering take on just about every part of the story. Once Emily had gotten over being indignant that I'd kept such an enormous secret from her, she was transfixed, her eyes practically popping right out of her head with each new revelation.

"So what you're saying," she breathed when I was finished, "is you saved the world?"

"Well, I—"

"I have the coolest best friend ever!"

I beamed at her. Lej, on the other hand, rolled his eyes. Pip, meanwhile, had found his way to Mum's knee, where he'd settled happily while she absently scratched his fluffy, feathery back. She looked like she was in shock. Meeting a boy from a sketchbook will do that to you, I suppose.

"Well," she said after a moment. "Well."

We waited.

"You must stay for dinner," she said. "I was going to make fried fish and mashed potatoes for the girls, but we have plenty of other options. What do you like to eat?"

"Everything," said Lej, and Pip nodded vigorously to make sure this point was not misunderstood.

"They didn't have the option of being picky when Mahishasura was around," I explained. Pip nodded again, this time with a look of piteous sorrow. Which was, frankly, a bit much for someone who had just stuffed himself with a cookie. If he'd had eyelashes, I had no doubt he would have batted them.

Mum's face immediately transformed. Hungry kids were her Achilles' heel. "I know just what you need," she announced, standing. "Come on, then. Everyone helps in this house."

She put the fish back into the fridge, pulled a hunk of beef out of the freezer ("Nothing says comfort food like a good stew," she said), and put the rest of us to work peeling and cutting up potatoes, onions, mushrooms, and a dizzying number of other veggies.

I was mid-potato when I remembered that Lej had never actually gotten around to telling me what kind of trouble the Kikiverse was in. I couldn't ask him now, either, with Mum right there in the kitchen with us.

Unfortunately, it was only a matter of time before *she* thought to ask why he was here. And she did, as we were eating.

"So, Lej," she said in a tone that I immediately

recognized as brimming with peril. "What brings you to our universe?"

"Lej came to get something," I said, before he could so much as open his mouth.

"Really?" Mum raised her eyebrows at him. "And that something wouldn't happen to be Kiki, would it?"

"Of course not," I said quickly. "He's here for the Wi-Fi."

There was a moment of stunned silence. Even Pip stopped eating long enough to stare at me.

"The Wi-Fi," Mum repeated.

"There's no internet in the Kikiverse," I babbled. "I put electricity and a double-decker bus and a bunch of other modern things into my made-up ancient world, but I didn't give them the internet. And it's not something I can create for them *now*, either, because, you know. It's the internet. It's impossibly huge."

"Is it really called the Kikiverse?" Emily asked.

"No, it is *not*," said Lej.

"You think you can carry the *internet* into the other world?" Mum asked him. "How, exactly?"

"Lej obviously didn't think it through," I offered,

shrugging like I was just embarrassed on my friend's behalf.

Lej glared at me.

Mum's eyebrows twitched together like maybe she was getting a headache, but then she watched Lej plow through his stew and her face softened. "Nevertheless," she said, "as it seems to be possible for you to carry things from our world into yours, why don't you take back a few things? Edible things, to be precise."

"Oh, we do actually have more than enough to eat these days," Lej told her. "It's just that it's not very good. Simha insists on doing all the cooking. You know the lion? He loves to cook, but I don't think cooking loves him back."

Out of the corner of my eye, I saw Emily mouth *Lion?* at my mother, who looked like she was, finally, at a loss.

"Did we not mention the lion?" I asked weakly.

"No," said Mum. "I don't believe you did."

After dinner, I announced loudly that it was time for Lej to return to the sketchbook. He opened his mouth, no doubt to point out that he wasn't going anywhere without me, but luckily, his good sense kicked in just in time and he kept quiet. So it was in total harmony that Mum and I crammed one of our old suitcases with fruit, chocolate, at least three million different types of cookies, a box of tea-bags, two boxes of cereal, an entire lettuce, those crackly candies that make popping noises in your mouth, a pile of books, my old handheld video games, and just about anything else we could fit.

Then we handed the suitcase over to Lej. I asked him to say hello to the others for me, Mum told him to take good care of himself, and we watched him vanish into my sketchbook.

"There!" I said, shutting the sketchbook while Mum and Emily stared at it like they couldn't believe their eyes. "Now that that's all done, can Emily and I stay up and watch a movie?"

"Not on a school night," Mum said automatically, just as she did every Tuesday. Just as I'd hoped she would.

After that, it was only about half an hour or so before the house settled down for the night. Emily, Pip, and I sequestered ourselves in my bedroom (with the door shut, obviously), Mum went to her study across the hall to get some work done (also with the door shut, thankfully!), and as soon as I felt like it was safe, I flipped my sketchbook back to the portrait of Lej.

He tumbled out of the page almost instantly. Without the suitcase, I noticed.

"Gah!" Emily yelped.

"See?" I said triumphantly to Lej. "It's an entirely appropriate reaction."

"Why's he back?" Emily asked, but the answer must have occurred to her, because her face lit up like twenty Christmases had arrived at once. "Are we up to something sneaky? *Please* say we are!"

"The Kikiverse is in trouble, and the Crows need my help," I explained.

Lej made a grumbly sound. "Stop calling it that!"

"It's growing on me," I replied tartly. "You should be happy. I'm embracing my 'entertaining' ego."

Pip fluttered down from the bookshelf and landed on Lej's shoulder, prodding him. Hard.

Lej sighed. "Fine, I'll let it go," he said to Pip, and then turned back to me. "So are you coming or not?"

"Are you actually expecting me to refuse? Or are you asking just to be obnoxious?"

He cracked a smile. "I think you bring out the worst in me."

"I think *you* bring out the worst in you," I retorted.

"Ahem," said Emily. "Can someone explain *why* Kiki's help is so desperately needed?"

"I, too, would like to know," I said.

Lej scuffed one foot against the carpeted floor. I noticed for the first time that he only had socks on. Clean, boring white socks. Where were his shoes? Not that I minded. We always took our shoes off as soon as we walked into the house. Tracking outside muck around someone's home was, as far as I was concerned, only *slightly* less offensive than murder.

Wait. Lej was talking about the Kikiverse. With some effort, I forced my brain to stop fixating on the shoe thing.

"Something isn't right," Lej was saying.

I blinked. "I need a little more than that, Lej."

"Well, you know how there's a river to the northeast of the city?"

"Believe it or not, I *do* know of the existence of the Kaveri, yes," I said. I picked up my sketchbook and pointed at one of my drawings of the river in question, mostly for

Emily's benefit. "I was there when we scattered Pip's ashes over it, remember?"

"Well, it's not there anymore."

I did a double take. "Sorry, what?"

"The river," said Lej, "has vanished."

3

Emily shrugged at me like this was one of the *less* weird things she'd been told today, but I was stunned.

"The whole river? How is that even possible?"

"We don't know," said Lej. "One day it was there, the next it was gone. *Poof.*"

"Rivers don't just up and vanish overnight, Lej!"

"Oh, they don't?" Emily asked. We all looked at her. "Sorry, I'm still trying to figure out the rules of the Kiki-verse."

"I wouldn't bother if I were you," said Lej. "She wasn't the best worldbuilder."

I let that one go. "Can we go back to the Kaveri, please? When did it disappear?"

"A few weeks ago. We've been trying to figure out what happened, but we haven't had any luck. And then it occurred to us that maybe *you* could bring the river back."

"What, like, with a pencil?" Emily asked. "You think Kiki might be able to draw a river back into existence?"

"She collapsed Mysore Palace with a pencil," Lej pointed out.

"I can try," I said. "But more importantly, is everyone okay?"

"Everyone's fine," said Lej. "For now. There's the whole Magicwood thing, but—"

"What's Magicwood?" I demanded, bewildered.

"You know what the Magicwood is," he said impatiently. "The huge, dark, enchanted forest on the other side of the river? The same forest where some of Mahishasura's army fled after the battle? You can't have forgotten all of that."

I didn't reply. Thanks to the way Mahishasura's celestial, otherworldly magic worked, there were a lot of things about the Kikiverse that I didn't know, but for some reason, *this* took me aback. Maybe it was because I'd always just called it the forest, or the enchanted forest, and while that hadn't exactly been a Proper Name with capital letters and everything, I'd just assumed that that was what it would always be called. But since I'd been gone, the Kikiverse had given it a Proper Name.

"Anyway," Lej continued, tugging my attention away from the odd, sticky feeling inside me, "there's something wrong with the Magicwood, but that's a problem for another day."

Oh, for heaven's sake. I opened my mouth to remind him that my brain didn't *have* the ability to shelve problems for another day and that, now that he had gone and mentioned it, I was undoubtedly going to obsess over whatever had befallen the forest.

But Lej must have seen what was coming, because he quickly went on: "So the reason everyone is fine is because the city doesn't actually get its water from the Kaveri. It gets it from the Old Well."

His tone made me frown. I felt like I was missing a piece of the puzzle.

I forced myself to ignore the big question mark over the Forest-That-Now-Had-a-Proper-Name. Silencing my very noisy brain had been impossible just a few months back, but talking to the doctor had helped. One of

Dr. Muzembe's ideas had been to give myself a quiet half hour every evening, during which time I was supposed to let myself obsess. Instead of trying to push away the ugly thoughts or stop the spiral of hypothetical horribleness, I was to use that thirty minutes to allow my brain to do whatever it wanted.

It had been terrifying and awful the first few times I'd tried it, but I had promised to give it a chance, so I'd kept trying, and it started to work. It was actually kind of satisfying to set a timer and then let my brain think all the weird, ugly, and nonsensical stuff that it wanted to. And, okay, it was hard to just stop altogether when the timer went off, and not-nice thoughts still intruded at other times of the day, but it felt like it was happening less. More importantly, when it *did* happen, it was now actually possible to wrestle my brain back under control because it knew it would have its thirty minutes of freedom later.

It was kind of like having a badly behaved puppy.

So even though I wanted to swat Lej with one of my bunny slippers for even mentioning the Magicwood, I was able to keep my attention on the peculiar absence of the river.

"What haven't you told me?" I asked Lej now, with more than a little suspicion.

He grimaced. "There was a rumor," he said, "that on the day we defeated Mahishasura, the gandaberunda was seen flying over the Kaveri."

"That's the protector of the kingdom, right?" Emily asked me. "The two-headed bird statue?"

I nodded. "But that makes no sense. The gandaberunda woke up to *help* us. Why would it make the only river in the kingdom vanish?"

"Because the city doesn't need it?" Emily suggested.

"The people might use the Old Well, but the river feeds the *land*," I explained. "So I don't understand why the gandaberunda would do such a thing."

"We don't know," said Lej. "I told you, we haven't been able to find any answers."

I bit the end of my thumbnail, trying to make sense of all the different pieces of the puzzle Lej had just presented me with. "Maybe that's what's wrong with the Magicwood?" I wondered. "Maybe it's withering and dying because the river's gone?"

"A withered forest wouldn't have a powerful Asura begging us for sanctuary," said Lej.

"Wait, what?"

"It's one of Mahishasura's former generals," said Lej. "He's one of the Asuras who escaped into the Magicwood after the battle. A few days ago, he surrendered himself to Chamundeshwari and asked for sanctuary."

"You're telling me there's something in the Magicwood that's *scarier* than a demon king's demon general?" I asked incredulously. "And you've decided that's a problem for another day?"

"Kiki," Lej said, his tone grim. "It's not our biggest problem. It hasn't rained since the day the Kaveri vanished. Not one drop."

"You didn't think to mention that first?" I demanded, reeling. "The Old Well will run dry without any rain! Everyone in the kingdom will *die*, Lej!"

"Why do you think I'm here?" he snapped. "We didn't know what else to do. We hoped that if you re-created the river, the rains would go back to normal, too. As for whatever's wrong with the Magicwood, we felt that could wait until we're not all on the brink of catastrophe. Besides," he added, "if there *is* something worse than an Asura general in the Magicwood, Chamundeshwari is probably a better match for it than you are."

"I'm new to all this," said Emily before I could think of a suitably sharp reply to Lej's last jibe, "but if a river has mysteriously vanished and the rains have mysteriously stopped, doesn't it sound like there could be something pretty sinister going on?"

"That did occur to us, yes." Lej crossed his arms tightly over his chest. "The kingdom feels wrong. It's not something I can describe. It's just a *feeling*. Like something's coming. Or like something's already there, but the worst is yet to come. It feels like . . . like . . ."

"Like a curse," I said softly.

"That's it. Like a curse."

I felt an alarming sense of déjà vu. When Ashwini had turned up asking for my help months ago, she had told me that fixing everything would be a simple matter of breaking a statue's eye.

Spoiler: it had not been that simple.

So it seemed very unlikely that redrawing the missing river would put an end to whatever new threat the Kiki-verse was facing.

But I had to try anyway.

"Okay," I said. "I'm not going on *this* adventure in my

pajamas, thank you very much, so let me get dressed and we can go."

"Your mum is going to kill you when she finds out," Emily pointed out.

"The last time I went to the Kikiverse, I came back at exactly the moment I left," I said. "I was there for days, but no time at all had passed here. Mum won't know I'm gone."

"Brilliant!" Emily jumped off the bed. "Then I'm coming, too."

"You can't," said Lej.

Emily's face fell. "What? Why not?"

"You're not keyed to the sketchbook," Lej said, like this was supposed to make sense to any of us. At our blank looks, he rolled his eyes. "Kiki created that universe, so she's the only one from *this* universe who can cross over to *that* universe."

"What about—"

"Powerful otherworldly deities don't count," Lej said irritably, correctly guessing that I was about to remind him that both Mahishasura and Vishnu had been able to cross to the other world.

A part of me was relieved that Emily couldn't come with me, because I didn't know if I could keep her safe and I was *not* going to lose anyone else, but I was also disappointed. It wasn't like opportunities to show your best friend the made-up magical kingdom you created came along every day!

"I'm sorry, Em," I said.

There was no relief on Emily's face, just disappointment. She expected this to be a fun, triumphant adventure, and she was sorry to be missing out. But she had never seen the shadow of a demon passing across the sun. She had never had claws dig deep into her shoulders. She had never watched her friend's neck crack. She had been told about the cruel, wicked monsters that had stalked the other universe, and she had also been told that the Crows and I had defeated them, so she wasn't afraid. The phrase *mortal peril* probably sounded silly and dramatic to her.

But maybe she was right. Maybe this time, there would be no monsters and no mortal peril.

"Oh!" Emily perked up a bit. "You could take your phone with you!"

Mum had gotten me a phone for my birthday last

month, but I thought it extremely unlikely that my data plan would stretch to making video calls from another universe.

When I pointed this out to Emily, she tsked. "But you could make actual *videos*, couldn't you? You could take pictures? And bring them back to show me?"

This was quite possibly the best idea she'd ever had. Why hadn't *I* thought of it?

So I faithfully promised Emily that I'd take my phone with me ("And your charger!" she said, sensible as always), and I reminded her that from *her* point of view, she wouldn't even have to wait long because of the whole time thing.

By this point, Lej's patience had worn thin, so I tiptoed down the hallway to get dressed and get my toothbrush out of the bathroom. I could hear the faint sound of music drifting through the closed door of Mum's office, so she was still busy with work.

When I got back to my room, I found Lej examining the set of picture frames on my bedroom wall. "This is your mother," he said, tapping one of the photographs. "Who's that with her?"

I emptied out my schoolbag, then glanced over. Lej's finger was on the face of a blond-haired, green-eyed man with a shy smile. "Oh, that's my dad. He was Scottish."

"You don't look like him. A little bit in the smile, maybe, but not much else."

No, I was all Kallira. Down to the nose.

I repacked my bag with a few spare clothes, a pack of melatonin, my favorite art supplies, a few other bits and bobs, and my phone.

"Did you know *your* parents?" I asked Lej, glancing across at him as I zipped up the bag.

"I'm glad I got to visit," Lej said, ignoring the question. "I like your mother."

I smiled. "I guess we *do* see eye to eye on something after all."

"We have a problem," Emily whispered. She was peering through the keyhole in my bedroom door, obviously feeling that, as she was about to be deprived of a proper adventure, *this* was her only opportunity to extract a bit of drama out of the situation. "Your mum's office door just opened. I think she's coming to check on us."

"Then we need to go now," said Lej.

He didn't give any of us time to reply. He just turned and

dove headfirst into the open sketchbook, which absorbed him like ink. With a caw and a shrug of his feathery shoulders, Pip followed him.

"See you in a minute," I said to Emily.

"Good luck!"

Then I grabbed my shoes and my schoolbag and jumped.

4

The first time I'd tumbled into the Kikiverse, the sun had been up, the stone beneath my hands and knees had been baked hot, and it had been so, so quiet. The hushed, nervous quiet of a kingdom that knows there are monsters around every corner.

This was an altogether different arrival. For one thing, this world seemed to exist in a time zone a few hours ahead of London, so the full moon was high, turning the turrets and balconies of my fanciful castle in the sky to a soft, dreamy silver. For another, it was *cold*. It wasn't quite frost-on-the-windows-at-night cold, like London had been, but it didn't feel far off. An icy wind nipped down from the hills and made my ears go numb in seconds.

But the biggest difference of all was the noise. The instant I landed on the other side of the tear between worlds, I was seized. Smothered.

Squished.

"KIKIIIIIIIIIIIIII!"

That high, unrestrained cry in my ear *had* to be Suki, and the second pair of arms wrapped around me could only belong to her sister, Samara. I considered protesting my imminent death by suffocation, but I decided instead to just put one arm around each twin and squish them right back.

"I'm so happy to see you!" I cried. I looked around, trying to get my bearings, and spotted Jojo in his wheelchair. I flung my arms around him. "I've missed you all!"

Before Jojo could do much more than hug me back, Pip, who had found himself a perch on one of the arms of Jojo's chair, opened his beak and said, in a completely normal and familiar Pip-ish voice, "And *I* have missed being able to speak!"

"Well, that's new," I said.

"Pip!" Suki squealed, seizing him in both hands and crushing him to her. "Oh, Pip!"

"Where *are* we?" I asked. The previous tear had

opened on a balcony above Pretty Corner Market, which was, well, a market on a rather pretty corner, but *this* was somewhere else. The floorboards beneath my feet were uneven and made of wood, we were definitely much higher than the balcony had been, and whatever we were standing on seemed to be circular, because it curved away and out of sight on both sides of us. "Are we at the top of a lighthouse? Is there even a lighthouse in the kingdom?"

"There is a lighthouse," said Lej. "It's on the rocks at the edge of Lake Lune. But that's not where we are."

"This is the tower," said Samara, her eyes shining. "You know, the structure that Mysore Palace reshaped itself into after you collapsed it? We're calling it Sentinel's Tower now. We're at the top. Well, almost. The gandaberunda's statue is just above us."

"The Good Witch opened the tear here, of all places?"

"She said this is where she could harness the most power. I guess it's because we're so close to the gandaberunda."

I knew I was there because something was wrong, but right then, all I felt was a warm, giddy joy at seeing the Crows again. They felt like home: the twins with their identical braids; Samara's hand reaching for mine; Lej rolling his eyes at Suki's raptures; Pip's merry laughter coming out of the beak of a bird; Jojo's quick, sweet smile and the starlight bouncing off his curly black hair.

The only Crow missing was Ashwini, and, well, that was complicated. I tried not to think about it.

"Come look!" Suki said to me, tugging my arm and towing me in the direction of the wooden balustrade that separated us from a *very* big drop.

The moonlit city stretched out below us. Back when this world had just existed in my sketchbook, and sometimes even after it had become real, I'd often thought of it as my golden kingdom. It was partly because of the way the sun seemed to turn the towers and rooftops of the city gold when it hit just right, but mostly it was figurative. It had been the golden, magical place I'd escaped to when I couldn't cope with my noisy, messy brain.

But it had never looked as extraordinary as it did now. The streetlamps cast a soft haze over the cobblestone streets and the winding train track below where, in spite of the late hour, the bright red train was chugging its way across the city. There were hundreds of lit windows in the boxy, jewel-colored houses. The faint, distant sounds of music and chatter drifted up to us, as if there were still people in the markets or out talking to their neighbors in the streets. When I breathed in, I could smell nothing but clean, soothing jasmine flowers and woodsmoke.

Gone was the fearful silence of Mahishasura's Mysore. This was a different city, a new city, one that was alive and hopeful and everything I had once wanted it so badly to be.

But that wasn't what Suki had indicated. She was pointing higher, at something far away, and I made my eyes follow the line of her finger. They traveled north over the rooftops and cobblestones, all the way to the jagged shadows of Chamundi Hills in the far distance, to the pale moonlit spikes of the Magicwood beside it, and then, finally, to the chasm between the city and the forest, where the bright, silver ribbon of the Kaveri River should have been.

There was nothing there. The river was gone, and there was just a cold, impossible emptiness in its place. Immediately, my eyes wanted to look away, like they knew that there was something treacherous about that void and they weren't about to wait for my brain to catch up.

"Wrongness," I said quietly, aware of Lej behind me. "You were right. It feels *wrong*."

It was quiet for a moment as we all searched that impossible chasm for a river that simply wasn't there. When I couldn't bear to look at it any longer, I turned back to the others. "How come people aren't more scared?" I asked, gesturing to the city below. "They must have noticed the river and the rains have gone, right? So how come the whole kingdom isn't in a panic?"

The Crows glanced at each other, their expressions decidedly shifty, like none of them wanted to be the one to answer.

Then, with a sigh, Lej said, "They think you're going to fix it."

Oh, great. My anxious, obsessive brain was going to *love* carrying the weight of an entire kingdom's hopes.

Again.

I tried to figure out what our next step needed to be. Should we go to Crow House and try to get some sleep before the new day? Or should we go straight to that terrible void in the distance and try to re-create the river? It was a straightforward choice, but it took me too long to make it because my mind kept flitting a thousand hypothetical steps ahead. What if it didn't work? What would happen if I failed the city that was relying on me to save it? Was I going to get the rest of the Crows killed, too?

Eyes straight ahead, Kiki. It was something Mum had said to me a lot when I was little and was constantly getting distracted by birds and buses and patterns in the pavement instead of watching where I was going, but I'd found it a surprisingly appropriate and helpful reminder lately.

I crossed my arms tightly over my chest, forcing myself back into the present. I needed a quiet minute to put my thoughts in some kind of order, so I said, "Okay, we might as well go find out whether I can use my one and only superpower to bring the Kaveri back. I want to see the gandaberunda first, but I'll follow the rest of you down."

Pip fluttered to my shoulder. "That doesn't include me, right?"

He felt warm and solid against my neck and cheek, but I nudged him away. "It absolutely includes you. Go on. I'm pretty sure Samara's been patiently waiting for her turn for a cuddle."

"You'll find a way to make this okay, you know."

I smiled. "You promise?"

"Cross my heart and hope to—"

"Pip!"

His laugh was full of mischief. "If a boy can't tell jokes about his own death, what *can* he tell jokes about?"

I watched him fly to join the others. They vanished to the right, so I turned left and followed the circling balustrade until the wooden floorboards beneath my feet started to tilt upward. This platform was like a snake, I realized, a gently sloping spiral ramp that wound its way from bottom to top around the exterior of Sentinel's Tower. That explained how Jojo had gotten up here in his chair, too.

There was less chaos inside my head. The cold air, the quiet, and a few slow breaths had helped. As long as I kept myself in the here and now, instead of letting myself jump hundreds of hypothetical steps ahead, I'd be okay.

At the top of the spiral stairway, if *stairway* was even the right word for what essentially amounted to a twisty slide, the wooden floorboards ended and gave way to a circular platform of smooth, creamy-white stone, the same stone the old palace had been made out of. There, on a pedestal, stood the tall, proud statue of the gandaberunda, the two-headed bird that had given Sentinel's Tower its name.

Each head was like an eagle's, haughty and majestic, and the creature's four gemstone eyes seemed to look down its beaks at me. As I approached the plinth, the statue stayed exactly where it was, but I could *feel* its heartbeat, a pulse of life that crackled in the air like electricity.

"What have you done?" I asked quietly.

The gandaberunda didn't answer.

"Tell me what happened. *Please.*"

No answer. I sighed, not sure what else I'd expected, and put a hand on its wing to say goodbye.

But the instant the bare skin of my hand touched the statue, I was somewhere else.

I could see a two-headed bird reflected in the water of a river. Wings spread, talons out, the gandaberunda soared over the Kaveri. Then it dropped low, talons skimming the surface of the water, and the water burst into blinding golden light.

Then came a flood of disjointed moments, like snapshots, too fast for me to make sense of—

—a shadow with slender shoulders and long, spiky antlers—

—a ruby crown—

—the clasped hands of a king and a witch—

—strange, ferocious creatures—

—an urn tipping over—

—a girl alone in the dark—

—an empty well—

—a dying city—

I jerked away and almost stumbled right off the pedestal. "What was that?" I asked, my voice shaky with shock. "What are you trying to tell me?"

No answer. Typical.

I took a deep, unsteady breath, and then, extremely reluctantly, put my hand to the statue again, bracing myself.

Nope. Nothing. It seemed the gandaberunda had no more to say.

"Great," I said with more than a little sarcasm. "Cryptic clues. How fun."

But now, at least, one thing was certain. The gandaberunda *had* done something to the Kaveri. The kingdom's protector had put the kingdom at risk.

I just didn't know why, or how to fix it.

The others were waiting for me at the bottom of the tower, where I staggered to a halt a few minutes later, more than a little out of breath after practically tumbling down the long, *long* spiral slope. I expected Lej to comment on my spectacular lack of athleticism, but, incredibly, he said nothing.

"The gandaberunda tried to tell me something," I said, sucking in dramatic gasps of air. "I need to sketch what it showed me before I forget anything."

"Is that safe?" Samara asked. "You can't draw anything in this universe without it coming to life."

Oh. Right. "Then one of you will have to do it for me."

"Bet you wish we'd brought your mum with us," Pip said.

"She would have been handy to have around right now," I admitted. "We'll make do. Jojo?"

He nodded, looking doubtful. "I'm better with patterns and fabric, but I can try."

"We'll take the train out of the city," said Lej, pointing down the long drive that led to the tower. At the other end, just visible between the lines of ashoka trees on either side of the drive, were the crooked gates, beyond which was Main Street Station. "We should have plenty of time to get something down on paper while we're on board."

As we made our way out to the cobblestones and streetlamps of Main Street, I looked back at the crooked gates, down the drive, all the way back to the moonlit Sentinel's Tower. I refused to believe that the gandaberunda, the sentinel of the city, had tried to hurt it.

So what, then, had it done? Why had it taken the river away if it meant no harm?

Something caught my eye and I paused, pivoting to get a better look. There were enormous swaths of vivid color on the white walls on both sides of the gates. "What is that?" I asked, trying to make some sense of what I was seeing. "It looks like graffiti."

"Graffiti?" Suki asked.

"Street art," I explained. "There's tons of it back home."

"Then, yes, that is what you would call graffiti," said Suki. She looked rather pleased for some reason. "It started appearing after we beat Mahishasura. I don't think it's just one person doing it. Lej spotted an old lady trotting away with an armful of spray paint one time, and Chamundeshwari saw a little boy a different time."

"So it's like a project anyone can contribute to? That's a nice idea." Then, as the colors started resolving themselves into very familiar shapes, I sucked in a sharp breath. "Wait. That's . . ."

"Us?" Pip said, fluffing his feathers proudly. No wonder Suki had looked so pleased. "Why, yes, I do believe it is."

The pictures weren't of *us*, exactly, but there was no doubt who they represented. There were a number of winged black crows, for one thing, interspersed with bright paintings of apples, swords, potions, pencils, lions, paintbrushes, and even a looping rainbow thread like the one I'd pulled off my pajamas to identify a hiding staircase. These were pieces of our story, and they had been painted here, for everyone to see, at the gates of the place where the demon king had been destroyed for good.

Other pieces of the story were missing, of course. After all, what painting could have captured the horrible, scratchy agony inside my brain that had led me out of the safety of Crow House and Pip to his death? What painting could have captured Lej telling me it should have been me who died, or Ashwini flying away on an Asura's back after confessing she'd betrayed us? These were parts of the story none of us wanted to talk about, and they would never be graffitied on walls, but they were never going to leave me, either. I thought about them every single day.

"If we're all done patting ourselves on the back, can we get moving?" That was Lej, predictably, but I was glad. My delight at the graffiti on the wall had turned dark and heavy so quickly, but Lej's impatient voice had interrupted me before I could lose myself to the inevitable spiral.

Eyes straight ahead, Kiki. I silently counted the number of fireflies I could see. This was another thing Dr. Muzembe had suggested: "Try to find something to keep yourself grounded in the present," she'd said. "You know how it's very hard to think straight when you stub your toe? That's because powerful stimuli have a remarkable way of blocking out everything else. I'm certainly not suggesting you stub your toe every time you want to break the spiral of your thoughts, but even something as simple as using a fidget toy or listing what you see can help."

It didn't always work, but sometimes was better than never.

Main Street Station was just across the street. Like all the other stations along the single railway line, it looked like a storybook cottage, all gabled windows and shingled roof, and its platform was a quaint porch jutting out behind the house.

We arrived on the platform just as the glossy red train chugged to a stop, its windows lit with warm light and its glass doors sliding open to invite us in. There was no one else in the car we chose, so Jojo found a spot for his chair in the aisle, and the rest of us piled into seats around a table.

As the train pulled away from the station and rattled its way north, I opened my schoolbag and pulled out the mini sketchbook and colored pencils I'd packed. I slid the pack of pencils over to Jojo and closed my eyes, summoning the strange, fleeting images I'd seen when I touched the gandaberunda.

"There were two hands, clasped at the wrists," I said, trying to conjure them back up. "One was dark brown and big, and the other was smaller and a much lighter brown. There was nothing distinctive about them, but I know they belonged to a king and a witch. I don't know how I know that.

"Then there was an urn. It was just a plain clay urn with a ring of gold at the narrowest part of the neck, but it was tipping over. I think that's important." I used my hands to illustrate the movement of the urn. I could hear the pencil scratching against the paper of the sketchbook. Nobody else spoke, but I could hear them breathing. "There was also a girl alone in the dark."

"A girl?" Suki asked. "What did she look like?"

"She was in the dark," I reminded her, opening my eyes. "She was young and she had long dark hair, but I couldn't see much else."

Jojo, having reasonably decided this was too nebulous to try to draw, simply wrote down the words *girl in the dark, long hair* and then said, "What else?"

"There were these strange, frightening creatures. They looked like big four-legged animals, like wolves or lions, but they were bluish and glowing and almost translucent, like they were made out of ice or crystal. And"—I swallowed, my throat dry—"there was this shadow. It was tall and slender. It stood on two legs, but it had hooves and antlers."

The twins looked at each other, eyes wide. Lej's

expression was grim. "Two-legged with hooves and antlers?" he said. "That sounds a lot like an Asura."

"Let's hope not," said Jojo, his brow furrowed in concentration as he bent over the sketchbook.

I watched him, frustrated beyond belief at not being able to translate what I was seeing in my head to the page, and interrupted frequently to say things like "No, a lighter, colder blue than that," and "The antlers were spikier," and "Not like that, it was more like this—"

"Oi!" Pip pecked at my hand before I could take the pencil from Jojo. "No one wants the scary antlered demon coming to life, thank you!"

"I'm going to pluck your feathers in your sleep," I said darkly.

"Hoo! I'd pay good money to see you reach me all the way up in my perch, small fry—"

"I'm not that short!"

"Were you two like this the whole time you were in the other world?" Lej demanded.

"I couldn't speak until I got back here," Pip reminded him, and then added thoughtfully, "But if I could have, I probably would have spent a lot of my time winding Kiki up."

"Ashwini used to say you were two halves of the same soul." Suki grinned. "Kiki's obviously the less annoying half."

Pip fluffed himself up and said, "That's because *I'm* the captain of—"

"—fun and tomfoolery," the rest of us said at exactly the same time.

Pip's eyes sparkled. "Well, I *am*."

"So you've mentioned once or twice," Jojo commented mildly. "Now stop pecking Kiki. I need her to tell me the rest."

"There was a crown, too," I said. "It wasn't a big, chunky crown. It was smaller and thinner, and it was a deep, vibrant red. It looked like it was made out of rubies. Lots of tiny rubies, with one bigger ruby set right in the middle, about this size"—I put my thumbs and index fingers together to make a teardrop shape that was about the size of a small fist—"with a crack down the middle."

Jojo did his best to re-create this, then looked up at me when I didn't say anything else. "Was that it?"

I hesitated before saying, "There was also an empty well. The Old Well. And a dying kingdom."

"Well, *that* part is easy enough," said Samara. "If the Old Well goes dry, the kingdom dies."

"But we knew that already," Lej said. "So why bother to tell you that?"

"To show me that it's all connected, I think," I said. "The gandaberunda was trying to tell me a story. All those things I saw are pieces of the story, and if we don't figure out what it all means and do something about it, the story ends with the death of the Kikiverse. And everyone in it."

There was silence the rest of the way.

5

Our stop was a tiny, isolated station by a narrow road flanked by paddy fields and veggie farms. The single streetlamp outside the station flickered like it was gasping for breath, but the high, bright moon shone like a coin and gave us plenty of light as we trooped down the road. Jojo stifled a yawn, but I was too cold and anxious to do much more than think longingly of my warm, soft bed.

It was, frankly, a much nicer thing to think about than any of the *other* things my brain kept drifting to. Like, say, the death of the Kikiverse.

Some of my hair had slipped out of the messy bun I'd pinned it up into, so I twisted a lock of it round and round my finger now, tugging and untwisting and twisting it again, trying to make it sit just *so* and finding that it never did. Like my ragged fingernails and my need to double- and triple-check that I'd locked the front door, my hair-tugging was what Dr. Muzembe called a compulsion. According to her, these were things I felt like I had to do to feel like I was in control. They were also things I was supposed to try *not* doing, but, well, that was easier said than done.

Pip fluttered to my shoulder. "We're here."

I'd started to refer to the empty chasm as the Void whenever I thought of it, capitalized and everything. Up close, it was even more unsettling than it had looked from all the way up in Sentinel's Tower. The empty riverbed was oppressively dark, an unnaturally quiet, simmering mass of shadows and smoke. The worst part was the way the shadows seemed to reach *out* of the Void, like long fingers, eating up the crumbling rocks, the dying earth, and anything else that was foolish enough to get too close.

Once again, it was almost impossible to keep looking at it. All my instincts demanded that I look away, that I *stay* away, but I forced myself to bury my fear as deep as it would go and kept walking.

"Jojo," said Lej. "Gogglers peeled."

I blinked. "What?"

"Eyes sharp," Lej translated. His jaw clenched. "Ashwini used to say it whenever we were out doing rebel things."

With a click of the mechanics in his chair, Jojo wheeled himself to higher ground and slipped what looked like a pair of clunky sunglasses over his eyes.

"They let him see in the dark," Suki said. "Lej made them."

"Good luck," Samara whispered to me. She turned and clambered quickly up to Jojo's spot. There, she opened a compartment beneath the seat of Jojo's wheelchair and pulled out another pair of glasses, a spellbook, a witch's wand, a bow, and a handful of arrows. She handed the bow and arrows to Jojo, put the second pair of goggles on, and knelt on the ground beside his chair with the wand in one hand and the book in front of her.

"Are you both witches now?" I asked Suki. My voice sounded too loud in the cold and quiet, but I was glad for it. Silence made the Void even eerier.

"I wish, but witches are born, not made," Suki replied, and the high pitch of her own voice told me she felt the same way. "But we're getting very good at using magic."

"The Good Witch never used a wand. Do witches even need them?"

"No, I don't think so. They make them and imbue them with a limited amount of magic so that people like us can use them to cast basic spells."

I turned to Lej. "I assume you want Jojo and Samara up there to keep an eye out for anything, um, dangerous."

He shrugged. "Can't be too careful."

"Come on, then," Pip said merrily, every bit as giddy and fearless a crow as he ever was a boy. He fluffed his feathers and took to the air. "Let's go get our river back!"

He flew right into the shadows. Swallowing, I followed him, Lej and Suki right behind me.

Once we were inside the Void, it wasn't as dark as I'd expected. Grayish moonlight filtered weakly through the shadows and smoke, giving me a reasonably clear view of the stones, moss, and cracked earth of the barren riverbed. We scrambled carefully down the sides of the riverbed to reach the floor, where I knelt to unpack a tube of bluish-silver paint and my largest paintbrush.

As I squeezed paint onto the stones of the riverbed, Lej and Suki came to stand on either side of me, their eyes searching the Void for the slightest threat. It was freezing cold this deep into the shadows, the kind of cold that went straight to my bones and made my teeth rattle together, and Pip must have realized this, because he came back to my shoulder and let the warmth of his feathers press against me. Even with his help, I could barely keep my hand from shaking as I dipped my brush into the puddle of paint.

I painted a few wide, experimental strokes across the stones, conjuring a picture of the vast, flowing, silvery water of the Kaveri in my mind as I did. I withdrew my brush, holding my breath as I watched the strokes I'd painted, waiting for them to transform and become the rivulets of water I could see inside my head.

Instead, the paint simply faded into the stone and vanished like it had never been there.

I wasn't exactly surprised, because I hadn't really expected this to work, but I wished it had. I wished it could have been that simple.

I opened my mouth to speak, to promise to help the Crows find another way, but Lej clamped a hand abruptly over my mouth.

"Look," he whispered.

There was something else in the Void. It was up on the

opposite riverbank, on the edge of the Magicwood, staring down at us. It glowed eerily, a pale, cold, blue-silver color, and it started to make its way down to the riverbed floor. It moved with the smooth, liquid grace of a cat, and as it came level with us, I saw that it looked like a cat, too. A *very* large, *very* wild cat.

In the next breath, there was a rumble of noise like a growl, and then another creature appeared over the top of the riverbank. It was also pale and glowing, but this one's ears were more pointed rather than rounded, its body heavier and more canine. My heart pounded.

"You know those big, glowing, four-legged animals you said the gandaberunda showed you?" Pip whispered. "I think we may have found them."

More like *they* had found *us*, but now was really not the moment for technicalities.

Moving his hand from my mouth to my shoulder, Lej pulled me to my feet. On my other side, Pip and Suki pressed close. I dropped the paintbrush. I didn't dare take my eyes off the glowing, menacing creatures for even an instant.

One of the creatures crouched, ready to jump.

Lej's voice was little more than a rasp as he gave us a short, precise order: "Run."

None of us needed telling twice. Pip snatched my schoolbag from the ground and flew up into the sky with it, giving me one less thing to hold as I bolted for the riverbank and started clambering up. Behind me, I could *feel* the breath of the creatures coming after us, white and icy like frost in the air.

I looked over my shoulder. Lej had turned and stood with his hands in fists, holding tiny knives between his knuckles like he had claws of his own, but the creatures *laughed* as they dodged him. One of them, the lioness-cat-thing, leaped right over his head, sailing through the air in a vicious streak of light.

Before I could even make it halfway to the top, something snatched at the bottom of my jeans and dragged me back. I let out a strangled cry as I tumbled, landing painfully on my back in the riverbed, all the breath knocked right out of me.

Ice spread across my body as a pair of impossibly cold, heavy paws landed on my shoulders, pinning me down. It was the cat-creature, its leonine jaws only inches from my face. Glittering eyes looked down into mine. I thought I might choke on how afraid I was, but I refused to look away. I had to be brave.

"Worldbuilder," the creature hissed, its voice high and cold. "Cursebreaker. You know not the foe you face."

My panic was too enormous for me to make sense of the creature's curiously old-fashioned turn of phrase, but one thing was perfectly clear.

"Cursebreaker?" I repeated. "So there *is* a curse?"

The creature gave me a look of disdain. "I had thought that to be obvious."

"But I couldn't bring the river back," I croaked. I wasn't sure why I was saying that, except that the creatures had only materialized after I'd tried to re-create the Kaveri, which made me think that maybe they were angry with me for trying. "So I haven't broken the curse."

"*Yet*," said the creature. "You cannot be permitted to keep trying. This game is between the kingdom and I, worldbuilder. You must be removed from play."

"And you're going to do that, I suppose," I said.

There was a laugh, which was little more than a puff of icy white breath. "You say that like it will be difficult," it hissed. "I already have you. You are prey."

"Actually," I said, a little apologetically, "I'm more like *bait*."

The cat-creature looked up, but it was too late. Jojo's arrow whistled right past my ear, horrifyingly close, and struck the creature's chest. Cracks spread out from the impact point, like a spiderweb, and the creature let out a single angry howl before its entire body shattered into thousands of tiny, glowing shards of light.

6

"Ow, ow, ow, ow," I said, feeling extremely sorry for myself.

"Stop wriggling and this'll go much faster," Lej said unsympathetically, plucking yet another tiny, crystalline shard of cat-creature out of my hair, a process that involved him tugging a *lot* at my throbbing head.

We were well away from the Void, waiting at the station for the train to take us back into the city. After Jojo had shot the cat, I'd staggered upright in time to see a golden ray of light from Samara's wand shatter the other creature. There had been no way to know if more were on their way, so we had left the Void with all possible haste.

"You did really well staying so still with that thing on top of you," Jojo said to me now.

I shuddered, trying not to think of how badly I'd wanted to thrash wildly and struggle to get free. I'd had to be brave, to trust Jojo and Samara, but they had come through, and we'd be safe in the warm, protective arms of Crow House soon.

As the train pulled in at last, Lej plucked out another glowing shard and held it up to the light. It had the same bluish, silvery shine as a diamond, but it was more translucent and felt much, much colder to the touch.

"I have no idea what it's made of," Lej said, following the rest of us into a train car. "It's clear and cold like ice, but it's keeping its shape in my hand."

"How are we going to get the river back?" Suki asked in a small voice. "It's clear now that this is a curse, but we don't know who cursed the kingdom or why or how to break it."

I ran my eyes over our small, shaken group. Jojo was shivering, Pip had huddled close to me, and the others all looked so unsure and worried. I found myself wishing Ashwini were with us. She would have known exactly what to say to make us feel better, to make us feel hopeful, and to make us fight harder than ever.

But she wasn't with us, and I couldn't take her place, but I could at least *try* to give us all what we needed.

"It's late," I said, and I was impressed by how calm I sounded. "I'm not going anywhere until this curse is broken and the kingdom is safe, so let's just go back to Crow House and get some sleep. None of us is going to get anything done while we're cold, hungry, and tired. In the morning, we'll figure out what to do next."

It was nothing like the comfort of Ashwini's merry optimism, but I didn't think I was imagining that the others' faces brightened a little.

We got off the train at Main Street Station and walked the rest of the way to Crow House. As we crossed the familiar cobblestone square with my Kiki-as-a-superhero statue in the middle, my heavy, anxious heart lifted. Across the square was a tall, crooked, mismatched house, rather like three unrelated tiers of cake piled on top of each other. It was the most beautiful thing I'd ever seen.

"Home," Suki said contentedly.

The front door swung open as we drew close, letting a long triangle of warm gold light spill out onto the cobblestones. It felt like a hug. In spite of everything that had just happened and everything I was afraid was still ahead of us, my face split into a smile.

"Hello, Crow House," I said, and I could have sworn the house said hello back.

It was quiet inside the house. "Where's Simha?" I asked, perplexed by the absence of the Crows' enormous feline caregiver.

"The trials," said Lej, starting up the stairs to his room.

"Trials?"

"For the Asuras of Mahishasura's army who were captured after the battle," he explained. "Chamundeshwari and Simha have been holding weekly trials for them ever since. Some are sentenced to imprisonment below the Summer Palace," he added before I could ask. "And the ones who did *really* terrible things are banished to the Nowhere Place."

These seemed like fair consequences to me, so I just nodded and said goodnight. The others had already melted away. Instead of going straight to bed like I wanted to, I went into the kitchen to take my melatonin, then dragged myself into a *very* speedy shower to wash the riverbed and any last slivers of cat-creature off me. There was a timer attached to the handle of the shower door, put there presumably to help us use as little water as possible. It was a grim reminder to me that I'd failed at the first hurdle.

Finally, I half crawled my way up two flights of stairs to the top floor of the house. There, wedged between Pip's old, untouched room and a new room that could only be Simha's, if the amount of forest foliage inside it was any indication, was the cozy room the house had made for me the last time I'd been here.

It was a little different now. In the last couple of months, as the weather in London had gotten cold, I'd decided I wasn't as into pastels and had taken a liking to Nordic patterns and warm colors instead. And Crow House obviously knew this. Lamplight gilded the soft carpet, the new fireplace, the paintings of constellations on the walls, the knotted-wood end table, the bed with its piles of soft pillows and Nordic duvet, the bursting bookshelf, and the desk packed with tidily organized art supplies. There was no clutter, no dust, and absolutely *no* tiny spiders hiding away in the ceiling corners.

"Hi, room," I said, the words punctuated by a yawn. "You're perfect."

I hung my bag neatly on a hook on the back of the door, clambered into bed, and fell straight asleep.

And woke to drool dried on my chin, crusty eyes, and a hand on my shoulder gently shaking me awake.

"Is it morning?" I mumbled.

"More like afternoon," said Samara, sounding amused. "We all slept in, don't worry."

As my brain and body shook off the last traces of sleep, I remembered that there was a curse to break.

But first, I needed to brush my teeth. One did not break curses and save kingdoms with crusty eyes and dried drool on one's chin.

Before I could so much as climb out of bed, however, an enormous lion loped into my room.

"Kiki!" Simha boomed, licking the drool right off my chin and replacing it with his own. "I cannot express how happy I am to see you! Are you well? Those dark circles under your eyes had me very concerned, but they seem to be more or less gone now."

I hugged him, wrapping my arms around his enormous furred shoulders and burying my face in his mane. "I missed you."

"And I, you." His deep voice rumbled all the way through

my body. "I only wish our reunion were under better circumstances."

"Simha just got back from the trials," Samara said, and added significantly, "which means Jojo and Suki made lunch."

So it was with considerable enthusiasm that we went into the kitchen to eat. Stuffing ourselves with brown rice, spicy chargrilled chicken, and too few veggies (in Simha's opinion), we took turns poring over Jojo's attempts to translate the visions the gandaberunda had shown me. We'd obviously already met the strange, ferocious, glowing animals I'd mentioned, but most of the other images were still a puzzle.

Then, her eyebrows pulled together in concentration, Samara pointed to the picture of the ruby diadem crown thingy and said, "I think I've seen a crown like this in a book."

"Do you have it here?" I asked, perking up.

She shook her head. "No, I'm sure I saw it very recently, and briefly. I've read all *my* books a hundred times, so I must have seen it in a book at the Ancient Library."

"The Ancient Library only reopened last month," Jojo

said to me. "When Mahishasura took over, the Keeper of the library was afraid the Asuras would destroy all the books and history there, so he sealed it shut."

"It was the one and only good thing to come out of Mahishasura's reign," Simha grumbled. "I was spared Numa's existence for ten years."

"Who's Numa?" I asked.

"The Keeper of the Ancient Library, or so he calls himself." Simha shook his big head like he was trying to rid himself of an extremely annoying fly. "He and I were classmates over fifty years ago, when we were both children at the School of Starlight in the gods' realm. He is my archnemesis. I loathe him from the very bottom of my heart."

We all just stared at him for a moment, somewhat startled by the unexpected turn the conversation had taken.

Suki was the first to recover. "Well, anyway, the minute the library reopened, Samara was right there waiting to rush in," she said with great pride and affection. "Geek."

"I would've done the same thing," I laughed. "And I'm *very* excited that we now have an excellent excuse to go visit the Ancient Library and find out more about this crown."

Lej took the sketchbook from Samara. "I keep coming back to this antlered shadow," he said grimly.

"Of course," I said. "Trust you to get stuck on the most alarming thing."

"I, for one, thought the glowing animals last night were pretty alarming, but I take your point."

"Okay, how about this?" I offered. "Samara, Pip, and I will go to the Ancient Library and see what we can find out. I'll use my phone to take pictures of Jojo's drawings so that we have a copy, and then that way the rest of you can keep the sketchbook while we're gone and try to figure out what these other images might represent."

"You can stop at the Summer Palace on your way back and visit Chamundeshwari," Simha added. "I know she is very eager to see you."

I felt a weight lift off me, the way it always did whenever I had a problem and knew how to solve it. Or, at least, how to *start* solving it. I didn't know if we would get any answers at the Ancient Library, but it was something to do, a way to *act*, and there was nothing my brain loved more than having a way to act on whatever was bothering it.

Lej, too, seemed relieved to have a next step. "We'll meet back here in time for dinner."

I ran back upstairs to get dressed, retrieving my jeans and plucking my favorite unicorn sweatshirt out of my bag. After last night, I wasn't taking any chances with the cold, wintry weather. Then I took a bunch of pictures of Jojo's sketches with my phone, stuffed it into the front pocket of my jeans, and went to join Samara and Pip outside Crow House.

"I feel like we should be singing a song right now," Pip remarked. "People always sing inspiring, happy songs when they set out on a quest."

"I don't think I know any of these people," Samara said a little dubiously.

"He doesn't, either," I assured her. "Disney princesses don't count."

Pip, who had grown very fond of animated movies in the months he'd spent with me in London, looked like this was possibly the most unforgivable thing I'd ever said. And, well, the sun was shining, the city was lively, and I was still happy about knowing what needed to be done next, so I obliged him by trying to come up with a suitably inspiring quest song. Soon, all three of us were singing off-key, stumbling our way through badly rhymed verses about daring heroes, wicked curses, and mysterious libraries.

All things considered, I felt pretty sorry for anyone who happened to be unlucky enough to pass by.

7

We hopped on the red double-decker bus at the closest stop and rode it to the Artists' Quarter, which was a few miles east of the old Mysore Palace and the new Sentinel's Tower.

The Artists' Quarter was all red-roofed, brick-fronted townhouses, balconies overflowing with flowers or easels, and arched brick bridges over canals narrow enough to jump over. I couldn't help noticing that the water levels of the canals, which were fed by the Old Well, were worryingly low.

At the heart of the quarter, looming majestically over the lively cobblestone square in front of it, was the Ancient Library. It resembled an enormous country house, like a few I'd seen in both England and India. Its walls were made of red and cream bricks, and its red gabled roof and two cheerful copper chimneys glowed in the sunlight. (Why did my library have chimneys? I don't know. I had liked the idea of them, so I drew them, and that had been that.)

"Before we go in," Samara said, "I should probably warn you that Numa, the Keeper, is a little, um, difficult."

I gave her a narrow-eyed look. Samara lived with Lej. How much worse could a librarian be?

Of course, this was the same librarian that Simha had called his archnemesis, so maybe that answered *that* question.

Then I noticed something odd. There were a handful of wide, whitewashed steps leading up to the open double doors of the library, and on either side of the steps were empty stone pedestals. I knew they hadn't been empty when I had first created the library—there had been two stone statues of lions on the pedestals in my first sketch, inspired by both Simha and by the lion statues in Trafalgar Square.

"Where are the lion statues?" I asked.

Samara winced. "Numa, um, had them removed. And dumped in the Forbidden Sea."

I couldn't quite decide whether to be indignant or amused. "So Simha was serious when he said they hated each other."

I loved old libraries. They weren't always the most pleasant experience because the dust inevitably made me sneeze, but I still stubbornly persisted in loving the smell of old paper, the crinkle of pages turning, the sight of shelves stacked with books, the sliding ladders. I loved it all.

So it was absolutely magical to walk into the Ancient Library and find all those things and more.

Golden shafts of sunlight streamed in through the windows, hitting the long wooden desks, the spiral stairways leading up to the second floor, the towering shelves and stacks of books, and even lighting up the dust motes so that they looked like sparkling fairy dust drifting through the air. The walls had the same red and cream bricks as they did on the outside, while the floorboards were of old, warm, creaky wood. I sneezed, just as I'd expected, but I didn't mind because it was so lovely in here. The only thing that could have possibly made it more perfect was a fireplace roaring merrily in a corner, but that was probably a terrible idea with so many old and fragile books around.

"Ahem," said a gruff voice from my left.

Like many things in the Kikiverse, I hadn't gotten as far as actually creating the librarians before Mahishasura had stolen my made-up universe from me. So, like many other things, the magic he had used to transform my sketchbook world into a real one had filled in the gaps. Which meant I had absolutely no idea who we were about to meet.

But of all the things I might have imagined, I absolutely, definitely did *not* expect a gargoyle.

"Kiki," said Samara, somewhat nervously, "this is Numa, the Keeper of the Ancient Library."

Numa was an actual, literal stone gargoyle, a skinny goblin-like creature with a turned-up snub nose, drooping pointed ears, a tweed coat, and an expression of supreme disdain on his face. He stood only a little taller than my knee, but he had clearly mastered the art of looking down his nose at someone taller. I wondered if he gave lessons.

"You're a gargoyle!" Pip said, astonished.

The gargoyle spared him one scathing look, as if he had far better things to do than waste his time on people who stated the obvious, and turned to me. "The architect, I see," he said, and it didn't sound like a compliment. "I suppose some would say I should consider it an honor that you have paid my library a visit."

"*I'm* the one who feels honored," I said, and it wasn't even a lie.

The gargoyle, Numa, looked slightly mollified. His clever black eyes looked me up and down. "You are here for a book, I presume?"

"We were hoping you might be able to help us," said Samara. She nodded to me, and I pulled my phone out of my pocket, opening up one of the pictures I'd taken of Jojo's sketch of the ruby crown. "I've seen this crown in one of the books here, but I can't remember which one it was. Do you know anything about it?"

Numa seemed to be more interested in my phone than in the photograph. He took it from me and started examining it from every angle, turning it this way and that with an expression of utter fascination on his face. After a few minutes of this, I risked clearing my throat.

With obvious reluctance, the gargoyle turned his attention to the actual crown.

"That crown is a myth," he said. "If it exists, and I very much doubt that it does, it has not been seen in a hundred years."

"But you know what it is?" I asked. "You know who it belonged to?"

"It is a *crown*," Numa said scornfully. "Surely even someone with a less superior intellect than mine can hazard a guess as to who it might have belonged to?"

I was starting to feel like maybe it wasn't such an honor to meet the Keeper of the Ancient Library after all.

"So you're saying it belonged to whichever king was ruling the Kingdom of Mysore a hundred years ago," I persisted.

With an impatient huff, Numa turned and trotted down one of the aisles of shelves, beckoning imperiously for us to follow. As we made our way past dizzyingly huge numbers of beautiful books and manuscripts, I attempted another question.

"It's still mind-boggling to me that I only created this world last summer," I said. "And yet Mahishasura ruled the kingdom for ten years before we defeated him, and the Crows have memories going back their whole lives, and now you're saying this crown was last seen a hundred years ago. Did Mahishasura's magic really create *all* that history?"

"When Mahishasura brought this world to life, it was an act of immense power," said Numa impatiently. "Yes, it wove an entire history into existence. Part of that history comes from details you added into your sketchbook, like the protection spell that made the old palace impassable. The rest was extrapolated."

"Extrapolated?"

"The missing pieces were filled in," Numa replied. "Which is to say that as far as everything outside of this world is concerned, none of this existed before you, our whimsical architect, created it. But *inside* this world, as far as *we* are concerned, we have always existed. Hasn't this been explained to you before?"

"Sort of, but it's a pretty incredible thing to wrap my head around," I said. We were climbing a set of spiral stairs, which took us past one of the tall windows. I paused to scan the city outside, taking in the red bus, the lamp-posts, the peculiar mixture of the old and the modern. "What year is it here?"

"This world was born from the imagination of a child," Numa scoffed. "It does not have a date."

"But dates must exist, or how would you know the crown hadn't been seen in a hundred years?"

"We don't use dates the way *you* think of dates," Numa clarified irritably. He jabbed a finger at Pip and Samara. "Ask those two. We measure the years by who rules us. Right now, for example, it is the First Year of the Reign of Chamundeshwari. Last year was the Tenth Year of the Reign of Mahishasura. And the year before *that*—"

"I think I get the idea."

"Will wonders never cease," said Numa.

"Calling him difficult was a bit of an understatement, wasn't it?" Pip muttered to Samara.

Numa found what he'd been looking for at last. He clambered nimbly up one of the sliding ladders to retrieve a thick, dusty tome and plopped it down on the nearest desk, using his knobbly gray fingers to turn to the right section.

"That's the picture I saw before!" Samara said excitedly, pointing at a watercolor illustration of the exact crown the gandaberunda had shown me. It was slender, studded with rubies, and looked much more like a coronet or tiara than like the big, clunky crowns I'd once seen at the Tower of London. "This is it, isn't it, Kiki?"

I nodded. "This is what I saw. A crown with tons of tiny rubies and one large ruby in the middle."

"A myth," Numa repeated. "According to the accounts in this book, this crown was first seen during the reign of King Mahindra II, was inherited by his son King Rohan, and then by *his* son King Jai. That was the last time it was ever seen. Of course," he added, sniffing, "these accounts are not at all reliable. There is no reputable evidence to suggest this particular crown ever existed. All the kings after King Jai wore the gold crown that you will have seen in countless paintings and portraits around the city."

"Weren't you around back then?" Pip asked.

Numa looked outraged. "I am old," he said sourly, "but not *that* old."

"Maybe it's not about the crown," I said, thinking it over. "One of the other things the gandaberunda showed me was a pair of hands clasped at the wrists. One was a witch's, but the other was a king's. Maybe the ruby crown was just a clue to point us to the *right* king."

Numa looked at me with a slightly more approving expression on his face, like I'd finally said something that qualified as clever enough for him. "Then the king you want is King Jai," he said. "There are very few records of his short-lived reign, and a great deal of mystery surrounding his life, so it stands to reason that he is the one you should look into."

"I don't understand how a king who lived a hundred years ago has anything to do with a curse that's been cast over the kingdom *today*," Samara objected. "But even if he does have something to do with it, how are we supposed to find out more if no one knows anything about him?"

"You mentioned a witch's hand as well, did you not?" Numa said to me. "Why not speak to the Good Witch? *I* may not have been alive a hundred years ago, but *she* was."

"I know she's been around a long time, but are you sure she's as old as that?" I asked doubtfully.

"She is indeed," said Numa with relish, shutting the ancient book with a very final thump. "A veritable old crone, that one. And who knows? Perhaps *hers* is the hand you saw in your vision."

After this, we decided to go back to Crow House and let the others know what we'd found out. Samara wanted to stay at the library and look for whatever little material existed about King Jai, so Pip and I left to catch the bus without her.

"What's going on with you?" Pip asked as we waited outside for the bus to arrive.

"Me? What do you mean?"

"All those questions about time and dates. It never used to bother you when parts of this world didn't make sense."

"It doesn't bother me now," I said defensively, but I wondered if it did.

"It shouldn't," said Pip bluntly. "Because this world may not be as perfectly stitched together as the one you came from, but it makes sense in all the ways that matter. Some might quibble with the fact that a lion from Indian folklore uses a microwave, and Numa might make faces about how this world came out of a child's imagination, but I know *you* and that's why it makes sense to *me*. This world is a mixture of the stories your mum told you when you were little and the real places you grew up in. It's all the parts of *you*, mapped across a whole universe."

"But it's growing away from me."

He blinked. I blinked, too. I hadn't expected that to come out of my mouth. I wasn't even sure I'd *thought* it until I'd just said it, but now that I *had* said it, I knew it was true. It curled up inside my heart like a cat making itself completely at home, a truth that wasn't going anywhere and that I had some very complicated feelings about.

"Whatever magic I have here, it wasn't enough to bring the river back," I said quietly, trying to find a way to put the feelings into words. "I guess I was trying not to think about it, but what if one day my magic just goes away completely? The Kikiverse exists on its own now. It has history I know nothing about! It has names for places and people and things that I didn't make up! What if it keeps growing and growing until one day it's nothing like the world I made?"

"*That* isn't possible," said Pip with certainty. "It might grow, and evolve, but it's always going to be the universe you put so much of your love, pain, and heart into. Mahishasura's power brought it to life, but you're the one who made it *live*." He nudged my cheek with the pointy end of his beak. "But it's totally okay to be a little sad that it's not the same place that used to exist only inside your head."

It was always such a relief to hear someone tell me that my feelings were okay, especially when they seemed *not* okay to me. It had taken me a long time to learn that I was allowed to feel big, ugly, not-nice emotions, and that it's the way we choose to *act* on our feelings that can sometimes be wrong, not the feelings themselves. Sometimes I still forgot that, but I knew I was lucky to have people like Mum and Pip to remind me.

Ashwini, too. I tried not to think about her because it still hurt so much, but she had been the first one to tell me that there was nothing wrong with the way my brain worked, that it was fine to be a little different and *more* than fine to ask for help when I needed it. I didn't know if I was ready to see or speak to her, but I wondered where she was. No matter what she'd done, I wanted her to be okay.

Bringing myself back to the present, I smiled and said, "I suppose the good thing about not knowing everything about this universe is that I still get to be surprised."

"I'm always a big fan of surprises," Pip agreed merrily. "Bet you wish there were fewer villains doing villainous things, though."

"I *definitely* wish that," I said with a sigh.

8

Back at Crow House, the others obviously hadn't had much luck with the rest of the pictures in the sketchbook. Suki and Simha were on the floor of the front room, playing one of the video games I'd packed in the suitcase Lej had brought over, while Jojo was at his sewing machine working on his newest project. Lej, being Lej, was brooding crankily over the sketchbook.

"Oh, you're back," Simha said, lifting his huge head. "Did you meet that ghastly gargoyle?"

"He was the *worst*," I said, which was something of an exaggeration, but I would have happily told much bigger lies for Simha.

He beamed at me. "Did you get a chance to visit Chamundeshwari?"

"Not yet. I wanted to come back here first to let you all know what we found out at the library."

Once I'd told them about the ruby crown, which may or may not have ever been real, and about the king whose life had been shrouded in mystery, Lej wanted to go find the Good Witch immediately.

"Didn't she open the tear for you?" I asked. "That was just yesterday. She can't have gone far."

"She's never where you expect her to be," said Lej, sounding extremely annoyed by that fact. "We didn't even see her when she opened the tear. She just did it and told Chamundeshwari, who then told us. So we'll have to go to the Witches' Guild and ask them where we can find her."

"Do we know where the Witches' Guild is these days?" The last time we'd tried to find them, it had been complicated.

He nodded. "They stopped hiding after Mahishasura fell, so that part's easy. They're not far from the Ancient Library, actually."

"Did you lose my sister, by the way?" Suki asked, glancing briefly up from the game and not sounding especially concerned. "Did she get gobbled up by a book again?"

"Again?" I demanded, wide-eyed.

"Some of the old books bite," said Suki cheerfully. "It was fine, one of the librarians fished her out."

I felt like I needed to know a whole lot more about this, but . . . one thing at a time. "Let's go to the Witches' Guild," I said to Lej.

This quest looked a little like a board game inside my head. As long as we kept moving forward, I was okay. I didn't want to stop because I was afraid that when I did, when our ideas ran out and we didn't have a next step to take, that was when my brain would start to do dangerously anxious, obsessive, and compulsive things, and, well, that was how Pip had ended up—

Eyes straight ahead, Kiki. My half hour of worry time wasn't until later. Every thought that wasn't going to help us break the curse and save the kingdom had to wait until then.

Pip yawned, stretching his wings out like he was human, and then fluttered to Lej's shoulder. He'd barely left *my* shoulder on the way back, so how he could possibly be tired was anyone's guess.

"I'll come, too," said Suki, relinquishing the video game to Simha. "I've been dying to visit the Witches' Guild."

"Jojo?" I asked.

"I think I'll stay and keep working on this," said Jojo. His dark eyes shone with excitement as he looked up from the sewing machine and added, "I'm trying to make fabric that can slow down time."

Jojo had made some pretty incredible things before, but this totally took the cake. "Is that even possible?"

"There's only one way to find out," he said, grinning. So he stayed at Crow House with Simha while the rest of us went back out to find the Good Witch.

"Why is it all the great quests always have so much to-ing and fro-ing?" I wondered as I got on the bus for the third time that day. "Can't they ever be simple, like go to Point A, find Mysterious Object, use Mysterious Object to defeat Wicked Villain, go home for dinner?"

"Maybe the next time you create a sketchbook kingdom, you could keep that in mind," Lej said unhelpfully.

By the time the bus trundled back into the Artists'

Quarter, Pip had fallen asleep on my shoulder. We passed the Ancient Library, where Samara was presumably still buried neck-deep in old books (Hopefully not literally!), and got off at a stop five minutes farther down the bus route.

If my (hazy) memory of the (somewhat vague and definitely impractical) map I'd penciled into my sketchbook was right, we were at the very edge of the Artists' Quarter, where the pretty, balconied, brick-fronted townhouses backed onto Lake Lune. From where we were standing, on the wide cobblestone street in front of the row of townhouses, with the early evening sunlight painting everything in shades of pink and gold, it was impossible to see the lake, but I knew it was there.

Lej marched up to one of the townhouses. It looked just like the others, with the warm brick exterior, a balcony on the middle floor covered in ivy and flowers, and a sloping roof with red tiles. But right before Lej reached the front door, it slammed open and a young woman with a long, wild tangle of dark pink hair stormed out.

"It is *possible*," she shouted over her shoulder at someone still inside the house, "that Her Epic Majesty, our beloved Saint Natasha, is not always right about everything! It is *possible* that I am completely fed up with the entire guild acting like she can do no wrong! It is even *possible—*"

But we were never destined to find out what else was possible, because at that moment, the young woman turned to face the street and spotted us.

As our eyes met, I realized I'd met her before. She was the young witch I'd once spoken to at the secret market in Tamarind Station, the one who had told me about the tracking spell Mahishasura could have forced the Good Witch to use to find me. Her hair hadn't been that pretty shade of pink then, but it was unmistakably her.

"Statue girl," she said now, the flushed red of her brown cheeks fading as she recovered from whatever had made her so cross. "Are you in need of a witch again?"

Before I could answer, another witch stomped out of the house. She was short and chubby, with her gray hair pinned up into a tidy bun and a pair of exasperated dark eyes set in a wrinkled, round, dark brown face. "Anya, you cannot keep storming off every time you don't like what you hear," she started, and then she, too, saw us and cut herself off. “Oh,” she went on, brightening. “It’s Kiki, isn’t it? How lovely to meet you. Are you just passing by, or did you want to come in?”

“We’d like to come in, please,” Suki said at once, obviously unwilling to have the conversation on the doorstep when the opportunity to see the actual Witches’ Guild was dangling right in front of her. I didn’t blame her. I very badly wanted to see the inside of that townhouse myself.

“Of course,” said the older witch, gesturing for us to follow her in. “Slayers of demon kings and friends of Natasha’s are always welcome to visit the guild.”

For just one moment, I wondered wildly how these witches knew my mother, whose name was Natasha, and why they thought I was her *friend* rather than her daughter. Then it occurred to me that there was no way they could know my mother, Natasha wasn’t an unusual name, and one of the Crows probably had a friend in the guild with that name.

I glanced at the young witch, Anya, who was rolling her eyes at the older witch’s back. I remembered what she’d been saying when she had stormed out of the house, about *Her Epic Majesty, our beloved Saint Natasha*, and I found myself incredibly curious about what the mysterious Natasha had done to annoy Anya so much.

Apparently deciding that her interest in our visit was stronger than her temper tantrum, Anya trailed back into the townhouse with us.

The Witches' Guild was everything I'd hoped it would be, and if the look on Suki's face was any indication, she felt the same way. The friendly, ordinary brick walls of the townhouse were crammed full of wonders inside. No matter where I looked, there was something to see: a fountain of melted chocolate flowing *up* instead of down; witches rushing past us with piles of books in their arms and squealing about being late for a lesson; a witch turning herself into a dove and back in the blink of an eye; cauldrons bubbling with concoctions; shelves crammed full of potion bottles; a small child curled up fast asleep in midair, a pair of neon-pink chickens clucking in a nest of clouds—

Suki looked like she'd walked into a dream. "Look at the cauldrons!" she squealed, her hands clenched tightly around my poor, bruised left arm. "Look at how many ingredients and *plants* they've got on the shelves! Kiki, LOOK AT THE—"

"You have a keen interest in the witching arts, I take it?" the older witch asked her, the creases around her eyes deepening in a smile. Even Anya was smiling.

Suki blushed a fiery red, but her enthusiasm bubbled out in a stream of almost unintelligible words as she said, "Well, sort of. My sister is much better than I am at using spellbooks, but I *love* plants and potions. I mostly just experiment, really, because no one's ever taught me, so the things I come up with are often a bit rough and *messy*. One of my potions did help Kiki get past the labyrinth of Mysore Palace, so that was cool! I also have a friend who likes to stitch magical ingredients into fabric and other materials. He's *so* talented."

"We would be very interested in seeing what you and your friend come up with," said the older witch kindly. "And in return for your generosity, we would be happy to share our knowledge with you. The Witches' Guild has always taken pride in our work with young, passionate non-magical people."

"Yes, please," Suki breathed. "We would love that, thank you! It would be the best thing that's ever—"

Lej cleared his throat loudly. "Much as I hate to interrupt—"

"That is a shameless lie," Suki said to the witches. "He loves to interrupt. He lives for it."

"We actually came here," Lej continued, undeterred, "to ask where we might be able to find the Good Witch."

Anya muttered something that sounded like *typical* under her breath, but the older witch just said, "Of course," and beckoned us over to the back door of the townhouse. She pushed it open, showing us a stunning view of the tiny pier, the docked fishing boats, and the sprawling golden-blue waters of Lake Lune.

The older witch pointed at something all the way on the opposite side of the lake. It was a white lighthouse on the rocks. "You'll find her there," she said. Her mouth flattened into an odd shape, like she was trying to find a nice way of saying something *not* nice. "I should warn you, though, that she is, ah, not predisposed to visitors at the moment."

"Hah!" Anya said, and then clamped her mouth shut as if restraining herself.

"Well, she's going to have to put up with us," I said, stepping outside. "Thank you for your help."

With a yawn and a caw, Pip left my shoulder and flew into the sky, stretching his wings. Lej followed me out of the house, but Suki hesitated for just a moment, glancing back with a wistful look on her face.

"You're welcome to stay a little while and see some more of our work," the older witch said to her.

Suki bit her lip. "Kiki, do you mind?"

"Of course not," I said. "We'll meet you back at Crow House tonight."

And so it was just Lej, Pip, and me as we made our way across the little pier and squinted across Lake Lune at the lighthouse.

"Is it just me," said Pip, flying back down to hover just above our heads, "or does it look like something funny's going on with that lighthouse?"

It wasn't just him. There was something peculiar about the water around it. Here, at this end of the lake, the water rippled and lapped lazily against the wooden beams of the pier and rocks of the shore. But *there*, it was like the lake had become a wild thing. It rose up in gleaming, sun-streaked waves around the rocks, lashing angrily at the base of the lighthouse.

"Maybe she's working on some kind of magic that's affecting the water," I said.

Lej's brows knitted. "The lake turned to salt water

around the same time the Kaveri vanished and the rains stopped," he said, gesturing to the row of docked fishing boats and the spotlessly clean, dry pier. It was only then that it occurred to me how odd it was that I couldn't smell fish on a pier and that there wasn't a single fishing boat out on the water. "Maybe the Good Witch is trying to find a way to transform the water back to the way it was."

I wondered how the Old Well had survived this curse. It was running low because there was no more rain, but the water inside it was still safe to drink and use in thousands of other ways. So how come the Old Well hadn't been poisoned like Lake Lune?

"If the whole of Lake Lune turned salty when the curse hit the kingdom," I said, "what happened to all the fish and the other creatures that lived here?"

"They floated to the top," said Lej grimly, and I shuddered at the thought of the entire lake bobbing with dead fish, "and had to be removed with huge trawling nets. I don't know what, if anything, has survived."

I rubbed my arms to ward off the cold. "Come on," I said. "The fastest way to the lighthouse is straight across the lake. Let's borrow one of these boats and get going."

We found a glum fisherman at one of the pubs near

the pier, and he gave us his blessing to use his boat, his expression transforming into something hopeful. I wanted to promise him that I'd fix everything, in part because I wanted to be able to promise *myself* that as well, but I couldn't bring myself to say the words out loud. I wasn't the same girl I'd been when I had first arrived in this universe, but the Kiki who always expected to fail was still a part of me, and her voice inside my head was still pretty loud.

Lej and I each took up an oar once we were in the fishing boat, and Pip was given the all-important task of making sure the sketchbook with all the drawings of the gandaberunda's vision stayed dry and safe. He did this by dropping it into the middle of the boat and sitting on it.

"Times like this," he said happily, flopping onto his back and basking in the setting sun like a pampered prince, "I really don't miss my human body. Imagine having to *row*."

We were barely halfway across the lake, my arms so achy they were entirely ready to fall right off, when I noticed that the waves of lashing, angry water weren't just around the lighthouse anymore.

They were, in fact, coming right at us.

And they were *huge*. Like the enormous, unrelenting waves of a tsunami, they towered so far above us that as they grew closer, they almost blocked out the sun.

"That's not good," Lej croaked. He reached over his shoulder for the gleaming hilt of the sword he almost always had strapped to his back and then paused and glanced at me. "How well do you think a sword will work on an unfriendly lake?"

"Not well," I said firmly. "Keep it where it is, or you'll probably lose it. Pip," I added sharply. "Get out of here."

Pip hopped to his feet, took one look at the tempest heading our way, and bolted into the sky with the sketch-book clutched in his talons. "I'll get help!" he shouted, and flew straight for the lighthouse, over the towering waves, probably to try to get the Good Witch to do some-thing about her spell.

My heart was pounding so loudly, it felt like it was going to burst right out of my chest. I was used to feeling afraid, with worry and fear being a constant companion of mine, but there was something especially horrible about the helplessness of being stuck in the middle of a lake with nowhere to go and no way to stop what was coming.

Then, unexpectedly, I felt a hand close over mine. I looked up.

"On three," Lej ordered, his longer fingers weaving tightly with mine, "we jump. Okay?"

I nodded.

"One," he said.

"Two," I croaked.

Together, we shouted, "Three!"

We jumped, just as the furious, lashing waves of the tempest crashed down on us, smashed the poor little fishing boat to splinters, and swallowed us whole.

9

There was a girl in the dark. It wasn't a frightening kind of dark, but it was a lonely one, the kind that's a little too quiet and a little too cold, and seems to have no beginning and no end. I could barely see her, the girl with long dark hair rippling around her, but I knew that she'd been alone until I came.

She turned her face to me. I couldn't see much of it, just her hair and dark eyes and a flash of teeth. I thought it was a smile at first, but I realized at once that that was wrong. I could *feel* her rage.

"What are you?" she asked curiously. It seemed an odd question to me. It wasn't Who *are you*, it was What *are you*.

"I'm a girl," I said. "Just like you."

She cocked her head like she didn't quite believe me. "Architect," she said. She sounded more like Simha, Chamundeshwari, and the Good Witch than the Crows, her accent more formal and Old World–y. "Worldbuilder."

"*Girl*," I repeated. For some reason, that seemed important. That I was Kiki, a girl. Not the architect, or the worldbuilder. Just Kiki.

"Have you come to help me?" she asked.

"I don't know who you are," I said. "I don't know how to help."

Her teeth flashed again. "Then get out."

And suddenly, I choked, gagging as grief, rage, and water seemed to fill me up from the *inside*, relentless and ice-cold, flooding my lungs, my mouth, my nose, until I couldn't breathe and could only clamp my free hand around my throat, choking and drowning.

Then I wasn't in the dark anymore. The girl and the dark were gone, and I was below the cold, angry, thrashing water of a saltwater lake. I thrashed back, panic engulfing me at once, and fought for the surface, but something was dragging me deeper.

I looked down and saw Lej. His head drooped and he wasn't moving, but I was still holding his hand. He was taller and heavier than me, and he was the one pulling me down to the bottom.

Let him go, said the part of my brain that I hated, the part that was full of ugly thoughts. *He'll get you both killed if you don't let go.*

No. Nope. Not a chance. I wasn't letting go. I *refused* to let go.

He'd have let you *go*, my brain replied.

Maybe that was true, but I wasn't so sure. This was the same part of my brain that told me I'd feel better if I just checked that the front door was locked *once* more, the same part of my brain that had convinced me to leave Crow House the day Pip had died. It told lies all the time.

And even if it was telling me the truth right now, it didn't matter what Lej would have done if he'd been in my place. I wasn't him. I was me, and I wasn't letting go, and I didn't have time to keep listening to my brain. So I thrashed at it the way I was thrashing against the water, and inch by inch, I started to swim upward.

The furious, freezing tempest in the water kept fighting me, and Lej's weight kept pulling me back, but I swam and I pulled and I swam some more.

On and on it went. Why was the surface so far away? My vision went dark at the corners, and my lungs choked on salt and cold. My arms grew sluggish.

Then, just when I was sure I'd given everything I had and I wouldn't be able to go any farther, help came.

Someone's hand speared right into the water, seized hold of the back of my sweatshirt, and tugged, yanking me up until Lej and I broke the surface at last.

I sucked in huge, tearful gulps of air and spat out a lot of words that I was pretty sure Mum would have been surprised to find out I knew. I looked around for my rescuer, but the hand on the back of my sweatshirt was gone, and there was no one in sight.

The jagged rocks of the shore were *so* close. I hauled Lej the rest of the way and didn't stop until we were both on dryish land at the foot of the lighthouse, soaking and shaking.

Then I let myself collapse into a tragic puddle of tears and snot and great big hacking coughs. I was not ashamed. I had earned this.

"Good heavens," said an unfamiliar voice, very posh and formal. "That is a *lot* of snot. Where do you keep it all?"

I pushed myself up to my knees and looked around. There was a man sitting on the rocks near us, but there was something very odd about him. When I'd seen him out of the corner of my eye, he looked perfectly normal, but when I looked at him straight on, it was like he went out of focus. He was so close and yet I felt like I couldn't quite get a sense of what he really looked like. I could see dark eyes, a longish nose, short black hair brushed neatly back from his forehead, a neatly trimmed black beard, dark brown skin, dark clothes, but they all combined into something . . . *blurry.*

But this was the Kikiverse, and this wasn't even among the top ten most peculiar things here, so I turned my attention back to Lej, who still lay limp on the rocks.

I leaned over him. There was a nasty cut above his left eyebrow. A piece of the splintered boat must have hit him there and knocked him out.

"Lej, wake up!" I said, panic and cold making my voice sharper than I'd meant it to be. My teeth chattered. "Lej!"

Nothing.

So I did something I'd been wanting to do for a very long time.

I punched him in the face.

"Gaaaaah!" I wailed, clutching my fist to my chest. Had I broken my hand? I was sure I'd broken my hand.

Lej choked up a mouthful of spit and salt water, groaning. "What was that for, you harpy?"

"Is your jaw made out of the same stone as your heart?" I yelled back. Why hadn't I just let him go when we were both drowning?

"What a touching friendship," said the man on the rocks.

Lej coughed and spat some more, then sat up and looked from me to the man. "Who's that?"

"I don't know," I admitted. I tried and failed again to see past the odd blurriness around him. "Are you the one who pulled us out of the water?"

"I may have been," said the man with a rather dejected shrug. "It is hard to say what I have or haven't been doing."

"Well," I said, a little taken aback. "Um. Then thank you."

"There is no need to thank me," he replied. "If I did

pull you out of the water, all I have done is condemn you to dwell even longer in this cold, cruel world."

I blinked. Lej stood. "Right," he said, his near-drowning having apparently exhausted what little patience he possessed. "Kiki, let's go."

With one last look at the peculiar man, I limped up the shore in Lej's wake, cradling my bruised hand. As we drew close to the lighthouse door, the back of my neck prickled, but when I looked back, the man wasn't watching us.

Then who was?

Decidedly ready for this day to be over, and only too aware that it wasn't, I followed Lej into the lighthouse and let out a dismayed, weary groan at the sight of the steep, crooked steps we'd have to take to get to the top.

"Thank you," Lej said gruffly, without looking at me. "For not letting me go."

"How do you know I didn't let you go?" I asked his back as he trudged up the steps ahead of me.

His shoulders lifted in a shrug. "Lucky guess."

When we reached the top of the lighthouse, we found that the Good Witch had made herself a study in a big circular room with glass walls. There were bookshelves, potion bottles, books on the floor, a sleeping creature in a glass terrarium of some sort, a quill that seemed to be writing by itself, a merry and blissfully warm fireplace, soft carpets, and an absurd number of throw pillows.

Standing by one of the walls and facing the lake, her back to us, was the Good Witch. As for Pip, he was there, too, flapping his feathers inside a hanging golden cage.

"Get Pip out of there right now!" I said, too indignant to remember my manners. "Is this why you didn't come help us? You were too busy locking Pip up instead?"

The Good Witch turned. She had dark brown hair that curled a little at the ends, a very Kallira-ish nose, and vivid purple eyes, and I was struck by how much she looked like a younger version of Mum. (A comparison Mum probably wouldn't have been too happy with, considering the Good Witch was apparently a whole century older than her!)

"Pip?" she said, raising perfect eyebrows. "Wasn't Pip the one who left us for the land of stars and honey?"

Lej was unimpressed with this euphemism. "Yes. And he is also right there. In a *cage*."

"Interesting," said the Good Witch. "I do not like crows.

I especially do not like crows who fly through my door without invitation."

But the golden cage dissolved into nothing, and Pip plummeted to the ground in surprise before recovering in time and flapping back into the air. Landing on the desk, he jabbed silently at his beak with one wing.

"You silenced him, too?" I asked in disbelief.

"Crows are noisy," said the Good Witch by way of explanation, but she waved a hand to undo her spell, and Pip immediately let out a shrill, petty caw just because he could.

I noticed that Lej and I were also suddenly completely dry. I was tempted to be grateful, but I suspected she'd done it mostly to keep us from dripping all over her carpets.

"Your spell could have killed us, you know," I said. "Whatever you did to the water, it almost drowned Lej and me."

She blinked at me. Once, twice. "My spell," she said slowly.

"The one that turned the lake into a tempest?"

She blinked some more. Then she said, "Kingfishers do not fly when the crescent moon spins clockwise."

"Oh, for flip's sake, not this *again*," Pip burst out. He

obviously hadn't recovered from the time we'd spent with her when we'd all been imprisoned in Lalith Mahal.

"I think you say stuff like that when you're buying yourself time," I said, noticing the way the Good Witch's shoulders had stiffened at my mentioning the spell. "I don't think any of it actually means anything at all, does it?"

"You," said the Good Witch, pointing at me, "are a menace. And I refuse to converse with you any longer."

"There's a curse on the kingdom!" I said, throwing my hands up in the air in exasperation. "And you're supposed to be over a hundred years old! Could you please act like it for five minutes?"

"Very well," she said. "*If* you address me by my name."

"The Good Witch?"

"That is not my *name*." Flopping ungracefully down on a sofa festooned with throw pillows and crossing her arms over her chest, she waited. "My real and true name, if you please."

"Very original, Rumpelstiltskin," I grumbled.

"I do not know who that is," she replied, "but I do know that it is definitely not me."

Lej looked like he wanted to murder her. Or possibly

me, because I was pretty sure he thought most things were my fault. "How are we supposed to just figure out your name?"

But I thought of how she looked a bit like my mother, and then I thought of the young witch Anya storming out of the Witches' Guild saying something about *Her Epic Majesty*, and I knew.

"Natasha," I said.

The Good Witch sat bolt upright. "How did you know that?"

I shrugged and said, "Blackbirds never sing when the sun turns clockwise."

Pip fell over on the desk, screeching with laughter. The corner of Lej's mouth twitched. I blinked innocently, waiting.

Eyeing us all with sulky disfavor, the Good Witch (*Natasha*, I reminded myself) let out a sigh and waved us grudgingly over to the other sofa. "Never let it be said that I went back on my word," she said. "What is it you need from me this time?"

"We need you to tell us about King Jai," I said.

Her eyes widened a fraction before she recovered,

but Pip had noticed it, too, and pounced at once. Literally. He pecked her shoulder. "You *do* know something!"

"Get away from me before I turn you into a feather duster," she retorted.

"Natasha," I said, emphasizing the syllables of her name. "I know you care about the Kikiverse. You opened the tear for me *because* you care, because you wanted me to come and help, didn't you? So why haven't you told anyone what you know?"

She set her jaw, every year of her age suddenly casting shadows all over her face, and said, "I know why the Kaveri is gone. I have seen it vanish before."

"When?"

"The curse first took hold when Jai was on the throne. I was just sixteen years old then." She crossed her arms tightly over her chest once more. "There was a powerful Asura who had a bitter grudge against Mahindra, Jai's grandfather. We only knew her as Sura. After losing her feud with Mahindra, she went into hiding to plot how she would punish him and his beloved kingdom. You know it took Mahishasura centuries to amass the kind of power he needed to break out of the Nowhere Place and transform a sketchbook universe into a real one, but Sura's curse didn't need anywhere near as much power as that. It only took her two generations to return and curse the kingdom."

I remembered the way the cold, glowing cat-creature in the void had pinned me down and hissed, *This game is between the kingdom and I, worldbuilder.* Had it been speaking with the voice of an ancient, vengeful Asura?

"So the curse is back?" I asked. "All this is Sura's doing? The rains stopping, the lake turning salty, the river vanishing?"

Natasha lifted her shoulders in the slightest shrug. "It is a cruel but effective way to destroy an entire nation."

"Okay, so how was the curse broken back then? Maybe we can do the same thing now."

"It has never been broken," said Natasha. "It has simply been held at bay for almost a hundred years."

Lej, Pip, and I glanced at each other, wide-eyed. "Sura's curse has been hanging over the kingdom this whole time?" Pip asked in disbelief. "But how? How has it been held at bay?"

Natasha stood abruptly and turned away from us, facing the lake below her glass walls. "King Jai had a daughter," she said. I couldn't see her expression, but her back was very stiff and straight. "A young, brave, and lovely princess. She was sixteen at the time, just like me. Her name was Kaveri."

"Oh." Understanding hit me square in the chest, knocking the breath right out of me. "The river was a *girl.*"

10

I should have figured this out a whole lot sooner. On one of our summer visits to Mum's childhood home in Bangalore, we had gone on a weekend trip to the real Mysore, from where we'd visited the real Chamundi Hills and the real Kaveri River. While Mum and Granny had stopped to talk to some old friends, Gramps had taken me down to the water and told me stories about the river.

In one, Kaveri had been a young princess who loved her home and people very much. When someone cursed her kingdom with a drought (I wasn't sure who, because that part wasn't very clear in my memory, most likely because I'd been distracted by something. A swan? An elephant? A speck of dirt on my toe? It could have been anything), she decided to turn into a river to save her people.

"Jai and Kaveri asked me to transform her into water, the kind of water that would keep flowing and flowing," Natasha said stiffly, still facing the lake. Her words were clipped and tight, like it was difficult to say each one. "She wanted to save us. I was young, but I was one of the last witches left with the kind of power a spell like that would require, so I did it. I turned Kaveri into a magical urn of water."

"The urn," I said to Lej and Pip, pointing at the sketchbook on Natasha's desk. "I saw the urn tipping over."

Natasha dipped her head in a nod. "The king and I poured the water into the dry riverbed," she said. "Sura's curse wasn't broken, but it was interrupted. The kingdom was saved."

"What about Kaveri?" Pip asked. "She's been a river this whole time?"

"Kaveri has been the only thing holding the curse at bay. Until now. Sura has been waiting, and now she has finally gotten what she has always wanted."

I couldn't believe there was a statue of *me* in the

square outside Crow House. There should have been one of Princess Kaveri instead. I couldn't wrap my mind around the kind of love and courage she must have possessed to spend *a hundred years* fighting off a curse. As a *river*.

The Kikiverse was so much bigger than me.

"Why did the curse come back?" asked Lej. He looked at Natasha, then at me, then back at her. "Why now?"

Natasha turned to face us. The last rays of the sun were behind her, turning her hair into a halo and leaving her face in shadow, so I couldn't quite see her expression as she said, "When the gandaberunda woke up to help us defeat Mahishasura, it did one more thing before it turned back to stone. It released Kaveri from the riverbed."

"It turned her back into a girl?"

"No, I am the only one who can transform her back. All the gandaberunda could do was give her a physical form and free her from the boundaries of the riverbed."

"But why did it do that?" I sounded angrier than I'd meant to, but I couldn't help it. I *was* angry. Why had the gandaberunda, the creature the kingdom trusted to protect it, done something that risked destroying it? It was a terrible betrayal, and I didn't understand it.

And maybe I was also angry because this wasn't the first time I'd been betrayed by someone I'd trusted.

"Now the curse is back," said Natasha, ignoring my question. "Kaveri is missing. And Sura will finally be able to watch the kingdom fall apart."

Something was bothering me, but I wasn't sure what it was. It felt like the Good Witch wasn't telling us everything, but then, when did she *ever* tell us everything?

"No, I don't get it," Lej said. "I mean, even if we ignore the fact that what the gandaberunda did makes absolutely zero sense, what *you're* saying makes no sense, either. You're saying the gandaberunda gave Kaveri a physical form, which is why the river vanished, but that doesn't explain why Kaveri didn't come straight to you? Wouldn't she have wanted you to undo what the gandaberunda did?"

Pip let out a yelp, clapping his wings over his beak. "Maybe she *couldn't*. The creatures that attacked Kiki at the Void must have been servants or inventions of Sura's, right? So what if Sura has captured Kaveri? To make sure she can't become a river and interrupt the curse again?"

I tried to piece it together. "The girl in the dark," I said slowly. "It's *her*. What if she's in the dark because Sura has her?"

Somehow, I'd seen her, in that heartbeat of a moment when I'd almost drowned. I'd seen the lonely, endless dark she'd been imprisoned in. I'd felt her rage, her grief, and her *fear*. She'd asked me to help her.

And I would.

I'd get her back.

"Did you ever see Sura?" Lej asked Natasha, taking the sketchbook from the desk. "Did she have antlers?"

"She is a stag Asura. Two-legged, with furred haunches, an armored tunic, and spiky, lethal antlers."

"Like this picture here?"

"I am not sure what that is supposed to be," Natasha said, eyeing poor Jojo's sketches with a very critical eye, "but the shape looks about right, yes."

So we had figured out the meaning of the glowing creatures (we'd had the dubious pleasure of meeting them already), the ruby crown (which connected both

King Mahindra and King Jai), the antlered shadow (Sura), the urn tipping over (the Good Witch's spell), and the girl in the dark (Kaveri). Other than the obvious empty well and dying city, what was left?

I replayed the gandaberunda's vision in my mind. All I could think of was that brief flash of the clasped hands of a king and a witch. Well, that was pretty clear, too, wasn't it? The hands obviously represented King Jai and Natasha. I wasn't sure why they were *clasped*, but maybe it was symbolic or something.

"How are we going to find Sura?" Pip asked Lej and me. "If she's stayed hidden for over a hundred years, she's probably pretty good at it."

"We'll figure it out," I said. "We have to."

"There are artifacts in the restricted and highly unsafe section of the Ancient Library," Natasha offered with the generous air of someone doing us a huge favor. "One of them is a piece of Sura's left antler, torn off during her battle with King Mahindra. If you can bring me that piece, I can use it to cast a tracking spell."

I thought of Numa, the gargoyle, and grimaced. "I think it's a pretty safe bet that the kingdom will literally crumble to dust before the Keeper of the Ancient

Library will let us remove an artifact from those hallowed halls."

Natasha let out an enormous sigh. "Then I suppose I shall have to meet you there tomorrow morning, whereupon I will cast the spell while we are still *within* those hallowed halls."

"Oh. Okay." I brightened. "Thanks!"

She looked pointedly at the door. "Until tomorrow, then."

"You're an absolute delight," Pip informed her, flying to my shoulder. "A real treat. I can't *wait* to spend some more time in your company."

Apparently immune to sarcasm, she only nodded seriously and said, "Many people feel the same way."

At the door, I paused and turned back as one last question occurred to me. "How come the Old Well hasn't been cursed this time around?"

"Because I enchanted it," said Natasha, the Good Witch of Mysore, in a stupendously smug tone of voice. "I couldn't protect every source of fresh water in the kingdom, but I knew the Old Well was the one thing that might keep us all alive for a little while when the curse came back. And I knew it *would* come back. Decades ago, I went to the Old

Well and placed protective enchantments on it so that Sura's curse wouldn't be able to touch it." She gave us a beatific smile. "You're welcome, by the way."

"We need to go right now," Pip said firmly in my ear, "or I *will* peck her nose off, I swear it."

11

Outside the lighthouse, I almost tripped right over someone sitting on the rocks in the scant light of the overcast night. It was the man from before, and he was still out of focus.

"Oh, hey!" said Pip, straightening abruptly on my shoulder. "A ghost!"

Lej and I stopped short.

"That's a ghost?" I demanded. "How do you know?"

Pip shrugged. "I just know. Maybe I can tell because I'm one, too? We're both sort of dead and sort of not."

"How entirely predictable," the ghost remarked glumly. "I cannot even do *death* right."

There was a moment of silence as we all tried (and

failed) to think of a way to respond to that. Eventually, I settled for: "What's your name?"

"Joy," he mumbled.

The sound of the waves crashing against the rocks made me wonder if I'd misheard him. "Joy?"

"Yes," he sighed. "Joy."

This was too much for Lej. "There has never been anyone in any universe less suited to the name *Joy*."

The ghost seemed puzzled. "Why is that? Is there something wrong with my name?"

Clearly at a loss for words, Lej said nothing.

"I feel terrible just leaving him here on his own," I whispered. "Let's ask him if he wants to come with us."

"Why?" Lej demanded, sounding slightly horrified at the idea of spending any more time in the ghost's company.

"Well, for one thing, he saved our lives," I pointed out. "For another, it would be unkind to just leave him here alone. And for a third, if he really *is* a ghost and is still hanging around here instead of going to wherever dead people go, maybe that's because he has some kind of unfinished business. We could help him."

"Oh, really? Because we don't already have enough to do?"

"What's *my* unfinished business?" Pip wanted to know.

"Friendship?" I suggested.

"Tomfoolery?" said Lej.

Pip fluffed his feathers in satisfaction. "Yes, let's go with that."

"Well?" I said to Lej, jerking my chin at the ghost.

He pulled a face but said grudgingly, "Fine."

"Joy," I said in a louder voice, delighted with this victory, "would you like to come with us? We're on a quest, and we could use all the help we can get."

"If I come with you, your quest will crumble to ash beneath my hands," he replied gloomily. "Everything I touch turns to dust and ruin."

"Well, you heard the man," said Lej. "Everything he touches turns to dust and ruin. Let's go."

I dug my heels in. "We are *not* going."

"Kiki," Pip said in my ear. "I know you're trying to be kind, but we have way more important things to do right now than try to convince a melodramatic ghost that he's better off with us than he is sitting here on these rocks for the rest of eternity."

He was right, of course, but I had to try one more time. I turned back to Joy and said the first thing I could think of: "Maybe it's time to prove to yourself that you *can* do something right."

There was a long pause as the ghost thought this over. Then, unfolding himself and rising gracefully to his feet, he said, "I suppose I don't have anything better to do at the moment, so I shall accompany you on your quest. Do not blame me when it all goes wrong."

"Oh, don't worry," said Lej, with a dark look in my direction. "It won't be *you* I blame, I promise."

I rolled my eyes but only said, "Okay, then, you two take Joy back to Crow House with you."

"While you go where, exactly?"

"I want to visit Chamundeshwari first, but I'll be back in time for dinner. Pinky promise."

Lej looked like he couldn't decide whether to be impressed or annoyed that I'd fought tooth and nail to adopt the gloomy ghost and then somehow saddled *him* with the pleasure of escorting it back home. He settled for sighing and saying, "Then you'll want to go *that* way," and pointed at a tiny cottage with the words LAKE LUNE TRAIN STATION printed on a signpost in front of it.

The three of them set off in the opposite direction, sensibly skirting around the lake instead of attempting to cross it again. Before heading for the train station, I bent down at the water's edge and picked up a small, jagged piece of wood, a washed-up part of the ill-fated fishing boat we'd used. With my trusty pencil and a resizing spell, I could probably re-create the boat using this piece of wood. It seemed like the least I could do for the fisherman.

Pocketing the piece of wood and tucking my hands under my armpits to keep them warm, I went to catch my train.

After we had defeated Mahishasura and Chamundeshwari had been crowned queen of Mysore ("Temporarily," she had insisted), there'd been a big question mark over where she would take up residence and rule from. Mysore Palace would have been the obvious choice, but it had become Sentinel's Tower, and no one had wanted to use Lalith Mahal after it had been Mahishasura's fortress for almost ten years, so that left only my castle in the sky or the Summer Palace. Chamundeshwari had chosen the latter, which was probably wise because the castle in the sky was a *little* hard to reach.

The Summer Palace was at the southernmost point of the city, a small fort on a bluff overlooking the endless, stormy Forbidden Sea. The real Mysore was nowhere near the coast, but I'd wanted a mysterious and dangerous sea when I'd first started sketching out a map of my golden kingdom, so I created one. I had absolutely no idea *why* it was dangerous and forbidden, because I hadn't gotten around to figuring it out before Mahishasura had taken over. I'd probably find out sooner or later. (I hoped it was later rather than sooner. I *really* wasn't up to fighting another battle with enchanted water today.)

Like the other palaces in this universe, there was a wide flagstone driveway for chariots and carriages leading up to a stone courtyard in front of the palace. Beautiful flowers grew on either side of the driveway, white and pink and peachy blossoms glowing in the lamplight. It was even colder here, the wind from the sea an icy, relentless thing, which was probably why this palace had been built to be used in the summer and *not* in midwinter.

The doors of the palace had been thrown wide open, but before I could reach them, a glorious figure with long black hair and a white toga-like dress came out to greet me.

Chamundeshwari's face broke into a smile. "I've been expecting you."

It was very odd to see her without her tidy warrior's braid and her armored tunic, but the warmth in her voice was exactly as I remembered it. She kissed me on both cheeks and then put her hands on my shoulders, studying me with the same kind of scrutiny Simha had subjected me to when we'd reunited.

"Good," she said. "You look better."

I grinned at how absurd that sounded. I'd almost *drowned* two hours ago, my hair was a straggly mess, and I was pretty sure there was still salt and icky lake goo crusted onto my clothes, but somehow she still thought I looked healthier and happier than I had when I'd last been in this universe. It was astonishing what a difference getting enough sleep—and some help—could make.

"So how's the whole queeny thing going?"

"The whole queeny thing?" she repeated, trying to sound stern and mostly failing. "As the person who left me to deal with the whole queeny thing, I'd think you might treat it with a *little* more gravity."

"I'd have been a very absent queen," I reminded her.

"True," she said, sighing. "And I take my responsibilities very seriously, but I am a warrior goddess without anyone to fight. It is most unsettling."

I laughed. "There's a curse!"

"And when it is possible to go to battle against a curse," she retorted, "feel free to come fetch me. Come." She steered me into the palace. "The nights may be safer now than they used to be, but it is much too cold for you to stand out here. Let us have tea before you go back to Crow House."

Over a steaming pot of jasmine tea and a plate of Mysore pak, I told her about the Ancient Library, the story of King Jai, the curse, and everything the Good Witch (*Natasha*. Her name was Natasha!) had told us about Princess Kaveri.

Chamundeshwari's face was grave, but it was probably a mark of how long she had been stuck doing boring queeny things that she actually perked up a little when I mentioned the demon Sura. "Now, *that*," she said, "is an enemy I can fight."

"We can't rescue Kaveri, restore the river, or break the curse if we can't find Sura," I said.

"Does Natasha know where Sura's lair may be?"

"It's kind of hard to tell what Natasha does or doesn't know," I said ruefully, and Chamundeshwari nodded, well aware of the Good Witch's irksome habit of sharing only a few pieces of information. "But she didn't give us any ideas other than suggesting the tracking spell." I swallowed my last mouthful of Mysore pak and added, "I was wondering if I could speak to one of the Asuras you have imprisoned here, actually."

Chamundeshwari lowered her cup. "I assume you're referring to the Asura general who begged me for sanctuary because he was so afraid of something in the Magicwood."

I nodded. "I don't know what Sura could have done to scare one of Mahishasura's most fearsome generals, but it seems like way too much of a coincidence that the river vanishes, a curse comes back, and a big, dangerous Asura is suddenly scared of something in the forest."

"I'll take you to him," she said, standing.

I followed her down a long, winding set of stone stairs. It got colder and colder, probably because we were going deep into the cliff itself. I'd spent way too much of my time on the London Underground worrying about the tunnels collapsing, so it was inevitable that as I followed Chamundeshwari down those stairs, I started to picture the Forbidden Sea pressed up against the cliff walls, breaking through the earth and stone and devouring me.

I never thought I'd be relieved to see an Asura, but I was. He was a very nice distraction.

The Asura general was huge like Mahishasura had been, at least seven feet tall, with an enormous human chest, shoulders and arms covered in a thick grayish hide, a wolf's head, and two powerful wolf legs covered in gray fur. He stood in the far corner of his prison cell, quiet and still and mostly in shadow, his greenish wolf eyes glittering at me.

"You," he said in a deep, rough voice full of malice and bitterness. "Trickster."

I'd been called a lot of things in the Kikiverse, but this was new. I actually kind of liked it, though I liked the angry way he'd said it a whole lot less. I glanced uneasily at the thick, solid bars between us, wondering how strong they were. I swallowed. "I wanted to ask you about what you saw in the forest," I said. It was so cold down here that my breath came out white when I spoke.

"I will not speak of it."

"But—"

"No!" the Asura growled, making me startle. "She will hear. I will *not* speak of her."

I gave Chamundeshwari a wide-eyed look. Just how scary *was* Sura? And could she really *hear* us?

"Everyone and everything in this universe will be destroyed if the curse isn't broken," I said carefully. "That includes you. I'm going to stop her, but I need to know how to find her and what to expect when I do."

"You need not concern yourself with that," said the Asura with a short, sharp laugh. "*She* will find *you*."

"Is she in the Magicwood? Do you remember where you saw her?" No response. "What did she do to you? Just tell me, please!"

In two strides, the Asura general was across the cell and right at the bars, his sharp, wolfish teeth gleaming in a snarl that rattled me all the way to the bone. I yelped. He grinned.

Chamundeshwari stared the Asura down and put an arm in front of me, nudging me a step back. "Answer our questions, general," she said firmly, "and you will receive a bushel of apples with your next meal."

The lure of the apples, an inexplicable weakness for

all wolf Asuras, did the trick. The general lowered his voice to a rumble, as if he was still afraid Sura would hear him somehow, and said, "I stumbled upon her in the Magicwood. Then, though I was on dry land, I was drowning. Have you ever come close to drowning, trickster child?"

"I have, actually," I said with a slightly shaky, slightly hysterical laugh.

"Then you know. I could not breathe. I stood on dry land, yet I was *drowning*. And all around me was darkness, an endless, endless darkness that I felt I would never be free of."

I shivered, thinking of how Sura must have trapped Kaveri in that same kind of darkness. I'd glimpsed it when I, too, had been drowning. "How did you get free?"

"I did not," said Mahishasura's general. "She let me go. And I fled from the Magicwood. Even now, even here, I am not safe. I see her teeth when I close my eyes." I stared at his own teeth, those shiny wolf teeth, and wondered again what kind of monster could possibly have made *him* so afraid. "You do not know what that darkness was like. I will endure anything as long as I do not have to endure that again."

There was nothing else he could tell us, so Chamundeshwari and I left. As we walked away, starting up the long flight of stairs, I couldn't help asking, "Don't they get cold down here?"

She gave me a long, thoughtful look, as if she were trying to work out why I cared one way or another whether the demons that had done so many terrible things were suffering. "Asuras do not feel the cold," she said. "Like me, they came from the heavens, where it is far, far colder than it ever gets here."

"You think it's stupid of me to be bothered by them feeling cold," I guessed.

"It is never, ever stupid to be kind," she said, and led me back up to the light.

12

The following morning, I woke up jumpy and jittery, wanting very much to hurry up and get on with what needed to be done (meeting the Good Witch so that she could cast her tracking spell) and also very much dreading what needed to be done (tracking down a powerful, vengeful, curse-wielding demon).

When I went down to the kitchen, it was still so early that the only one awake was Jojo, who looked sheepishly up at me from the table because he was halfway through what looked like his third bowl of Special Flakes.

"Of all the things I thought you lot would go wild for," I said, amused, "I have to admit basic supermarket cereal was not it."

"Basic? It says 'special' right here on the box!"

I got the milk out of the fridge and sat down across from him. "Have you figured out time travel yet?"

"No," he said with a smile, too even-tempered and too used to living with Suki and Pip to be riled by my teasing. "But seeing as I was never trying to figure out *time travel*, I'm not too disappointed. If, on the other hand, you want to know whether I figured out how to make fabric that can *slow time down*, then I might have a different answer for you."

"Did you?" I asked, so distracted by this that I didn't notice how much milk I was pouring into my bowl of cereal.

He took the milk out of my hands. Really, he was too sensible for this household. "Almost."

"Seriously?"

"Is that doubt I hear in your voice, Kiki Kallira?"

"I never doubt *you*," I said at once, making him grin. "I just doubt timey stuff."

Jojo raised one eyebrow. "Timey stuff?"

"Timey stuff," I said firmly. "That's the proper name and everything."

Laughing, he held the milk back out to me. I reached

for it, but he didn't let go. He had gone very still all of a sudden. I followed the direction of his eyes. He was staring at my wrist.

I turned my arm over. There was a weird mark on the inside of my wrist, not even an inch wide: three gold lines, crisscrossing each other to make the shape of a triangle.

"This wasn't here when I was in London," I said, bewildered. I rubbed my left thumb against the mark, but it wouldn't budge. I licked my thumb and tried again, but it stayed put. "What *is* this? Where did it come from?"

"Look," Jojo said in an odd voice. He used both arms to lift his left leg, tugged up the bottom of his jeans, and showed me an identical gold tattoo on his ankle.

"Have you *all* got one?" I asked.

He nodded. "Suki was the first one to find hers, then Samara, then me. Lej discovered his just a couple of weeks ago. They don't come off, no matter how hard you scrub, but they don't do anything else, either. They're just *there*."

"But where did they come from?"

"We don't know," said Jojo. "The only thing we've been able to figure out is that each of our tattoos turned up after we went somewhere with a lot of other people, like the market or the bus. Did anyone touch you when you were out yesterday?"

"Probably," I said, wide-eyed. "I went all over the city yesterday and probably bumped into tons of people." Then something alarming occurred to me. "But if that's really how this happened, that would suggest someone *did* this to us. That there's someone out there who has been catching us when we're not paying attention and placing some kind of tattoo on our skin!"

"Weird, right?"

"It's downright creepy, is what it is! What if it's part of the curse?"

Jojo's brows furrowed. "Suki found her tattoo awhile after the Kaveri vanished, so I guess they *could* be connected somehow." He tapped his spoon absentmindedly against his empty bowl, thinking. "If that's the case, why haven't the tattoos done anything to us?"

"Maybe," I said, a chill skittering down my spine, "they just haven't done anything *yet*."

Thanks so much, said my brain. *I really needed something else to worry about.*

At that moment, Lej strode into the kitchen, muttered a groggy hello to the room, and plucked a handful of grapes out of the fruit bowl on the counter. He was wearing jeans and what seemed to be the top half of the rainbow unicorn pajamas I'd made him before I'd left the Kikiverse last time. He also had his boring white socks on, which meant he was about to go out.

"Where are you going?" Jojo asked the question before I could.

"I want to stop by the workshop before we go to the Ancient Library."

I twisted in my chair to look at him. "The metalworkers' workshop? The one you went to when we were trying to find a way to get to the top of Mysore Palace?"

"Yes," said Lej warily.

"Can I come with you?"

He glanced briefly up at the ceiling, as if asking some higher being what he had done to deserve my continued presence in his life. "Only if you're at the front door in exactly two minutes."

"I don't need two minutes," I said victoriously. "I'm already dressed."

He looked doubtfully at my striped rainbow leggings and the lavender romper I'd put on over them. "If you say so."

"If you need a coat, one of Ashwini's jackets is still on the hook by the front door," Jojo said to me.

I didn't want to borrow one of Ashwini's jackets, because that would make me think of her every single time I glanced down at myself and saw it, but my sweatshirt from the previous day was still crusty with lake salt and I hadn't packed any other warm clothes, so it was unavoidable.

Thankfully, it was a plain black jacket with one of those warm sheepskin linings. I wasn't sure I would've been able to bring myself to wear the red leather jacket Ashwini had worn all the time. She probably still had it.

Lej was already halfway across the square by the time I'd shoved my feet into my shoes, so I jogged after him to catch up.

I expected him to stay grim and silent the whole walk to the metalworkers' workshop. When I'd gotten back to Crow House the previous night, Lej had made it clear that he was never, ever going to forgive me for adopting a glum ghost and then abandoning him with it.

But to my surprise, Lej spoke first. "If we find Sura, what then?"

There were a lot of things I liked about Lej (okay, maybe not a *lot*, but definitely a few), but this was not one of them. When he asked me questions like that, I could always hear something in his voice, like he was testing me. Like he *wanted* me to say the wrong thing so that he could then get annoyed and say, *See? We obviously don't need you if you're going to come up with nonsense like that.*

I wasn't exactly sure he would be wrong, either. Wasn't the Kikiverse growing without me? So *did* they need me? It wasn't like *I* could fight Sura. I'd beaten Mahishasura with bravery and trickery, both of which I was proud of, but neither would get me past Sura's glowing, ferocious creatures or whatever dreadful power she possessed that had sent a fearsome Asura general fleeing from the Magicwood. Lej had come to London to ask for my help because the Crows had hoped I'd be able to re-create the river, but whatever mysterious worldbuilder magic I had in this universe hadn't been powerful enough to break the curse. And the gandaberunda's vision, which had been shown only to me, was now deciphered and understood. So what use was I? That was probably the question Lej was asking himself, just as he'd asked it of me right before I had gone and gotten Pip killed.

"Kiki?"

I blinked. Lej's eyebrows had pulled together in a frown. As usual, my thoughts had hopped and jumped many, many steps ahead of the present. I hadn't answered Lej's question. He hadn't scoffed at my answer. No one had told me they didn't need me. No one had blamed me for Pip. (Well, *I* had, but I was used to that.)

So instead of letting the conversation play out like I'd imagined it, I decided to be honest. "I wish you wouldn't ask me questions like you're hoping I give you the wrong answer."

"That's not what—" Lej stopped, biting off both the defensive reply and the sharp tone of his voice. Like me, he had some bad habits. After a second's pause, he went on in a gruffer, quieter voice, "I've asked you questions like that before, which wasn't fair. Sorry. I really didn't mean it that way this time."

I let out a breath, both surprised and relieved that we'd avoided biting each other's heads off. "I don't have a real plan," I said. "But Chamundeshwari is dying to go to battle, and she and Simha are definitely the best warriors we know, so I was thinking maybe we could ask them to distract Sura while the rest of us try to find and free Kaveri."

"Could work," said Lej. "The only thing is, Sura might have a lot more of those glowing beasts."

I nodded. "That's what I'm worried about. We need a Plan B just in case."

So that was what we brainstormed for the rest of the walk to the workshop, trading increasingly useless ideas until we came to stop on a lively street crammed with woodshops, spice shops, and craft shops. Perched on one corner was the crooked, blocky shape of the workshop we wanted.

There was a wooden sign hanging outside the front door, with the words NOT OPEN BEFORE NOON, GO AWAY! painted on it in very stern block letters, but Lej ignored the sign entirely and walked into the workshop. Feeling horribly rude, I followed.

"Dev!" Lej yelled as we entered what looked like a quaint shop front crammed with metal gears and whirring fidgets. I almost tripped over a small robot that seemed to be sweeping dust and debris off the wooden floor. "Archie!"

The robot, which was so small it didn't even reach my knee, paused its sweeping to look up at me. It had a little square metal face, expressionless apart from a pair of blinking, clicking silver eyes that made me think of a hopeful puppy.

"Um," I said, not quite sure how one was supposed to talk to robots. "You're doing such a great job."

Looking pleased, the robot went enthusiastically back to work.

We hadn't been there more than a moment or two when a shock of white hair, a wrinkled face, and a wide, toothy smile popped out of an open doorway at the other end of the shop front.

"Lej!" the newcomer cried, showing more delight than I'd ever seen anyone display at the sight of Lej. "How are you, darling boy? I was just saying to Archie that it had been a while since we'd seen you, wasn't I, Archie? Archie? Now, where's that man gone? I was sure he was right behind me. He said he needed a chisel from in here. Though why he might need a chisel, of all things, is a mystery, when you know he can't tell a chisel from a Chihuahua. And to think he calls *me* featherbrained. Can you believe it? And while we're on the subject, Lej, I must tell you about my latest idea for improvements to—"

"Dev," Lej said in the firm voice of someone who had had to interrupt similar speeches many times before. "I brought someone to see you."

Dev took one look at me and let out a scream that almost made my ears bleed. "Archie!" he howled. *"Archie!"*

Another man arrived. "What's that?" he shouted, in the way elderly people sometimes did because they couldn't hear very well. He was, somehow, even older than Dev. He had a walking stick, wisps of white hair lying flat on his head, and what looked like a metal toy engine in his free hand. He peered at us over the top of his gold-rimmed glasses. "Is that Lej? Has he explained why he hasn't come to visit in weeks?"

"Never mind Lej!" Dev said excitedly, and I choked on a laugh at Lej's expression. "Look! Look who he's brought with him!"

I waved.

"That's Archan," Lej said to me under his breath. "Archie."

Archie blinked owlishly at me.

Dev lost patience. "It's Kiki! Lej brought Kiki Kallira!"

"Don't be ridiculous," said Archie firmly.

"He did."

"That girl is not Kiki."

Dev stamped his foot. "Put your glasses on properly and look!"

Archie made a huffing sound but pushed his glasses up his nose. He blinked at me some more. Then he said, "Have you broken the curse yet?"

"Um. Not quite."

"Speak up, girl!"

"*Any day now*!" I shouted.

"Excellent," said Archie cheerfully. He tucked his walking stick and the toy engine under one armpit and used his newly freed hands to pinch my cheeks. "A good, trustworthy face. I'm glad Lej brought you. I told you we could count on Lej, didn't I, Dev?"

"No, *I* told *you* we could count on Lej—"

"How about one or both of you count your way to my wings?" Lej interrupted with the kind of impudence only a beloved grandchild can usually get away with. "I might need them if we're going to be breaking curses and all that."

Dev clapped his hands together happily. He checked the pocket of his tartan button-down shirt, like he thought he might have stashed the wings in there, and fished out a very small guinea pig instead. "Here, you hold Pandhi while I fetch the wings," he said, thrusting the animal at me. "Don't let him get cold!"

I held the sleeping guinea pig doubtfully to my chest. "'Pandhi,'" I said to Lej, repeating what Dev had called the little piglet. "Isn't that the Kodava word for—"

"'Pork'?" said Lej, grinning. "Yep."

I sputtered a horrified laugh and clutched the guinea pig tighter to my chest. "No one's going to turn you to bacon," I assured him. "You're much too sweet and cute for that, aren't you?"

Pandhi woke long enough to bite my finger and went promptly back to sleep.

"That's what I get for being nice," I said bitterly to Lej, who was laughing out loud for maybe the fifth time in his entire life. "Take him before I'm tempted to feed him to Pip."

Across the room, Archie had bent down to pat the little sweeping robot on the head. "It's one of the first things I ever made! It's going on seventy-odd years old now, bless it. Your visit seems to have perked it up."

Dev skipped back into the room, a pair of sleek, folded metal wings in his arms. "New and improved," he said proudly, handing them to Lej, who immediately traded the guinea pig for the wings. "Some of your ideas didn't work out, but the others were splendid, weren't they, Archie? I think you'll find these are much lighter, much more comfortable, and much more powerful. If they work like we hope, we'll make more for the other Crows. Oh, if we could only go with you on your adventure! What a thrill it would be, wouldn't it, Archie? *Archie!*"

Archie had gone to sleep with his chin propped on his walking stick.

"Typical," said Dev.

"Do you want me to carry him to his bed?" Lej asked.

"No need," said Dev. "He's like a cat, napping in fits and starts all day." He popped the guinea pig back into his pocket and followed us to the door. "Now, Lej, don't leave it so long before your next visit. You know how much we love having you here. And Kiki, what a pleasure it has been to meet you! Good luck!"

I raised my eyebrows at Lej, grinning. "Someone actually loves having you around?"

"Shut up."

I waited until we were out of earshot of the workshop before asking my next question. "You're really trying the whole wing thing again?" The last time Lej had tried using a pair of crafted metal wings, they had been clunky, the mechanics hadn't worked properly, and he'd almost plummeted to his death before managing to make it safely to the top of Mysore Palace.

"These are better than the last ones," Lej said defensively.

I closed my eyes to shut out the thought of him falling out of the sky, but of course that picture was *inside* my brain, so it didn't go anywhere. "I do *not* like worrying about you."

"Open your eyes before you fall flat on your face and I have to explain your broken nose to your mother" was the only reply I got.

13

With the exception of Jojo and Joy (who had decided to stay behind at Crow House because he was terrified of frogs, water, and most of all, witches), we were all outside the Ancient Library an hour later, waiting for the predictably unpunctual Good Witch.

Simha paced at the foot of the steps, glowering at the empty pedestals where the lion statues had once stood. Nearby, the twins giggled at the sight of Pip trying to see how long he could get away with making himself a nest in Lej's hair before getting unceremoniously brushed off.

Not long, it turned out.

I would have enjoyed these shenanigans, too, but I

was too preoccupied with how different the atmosphere in the city was today. Yesterday, it had been alive and busy, full of noise and color, and the people I had spoken to in passing had been cheerful. Today, the streets were emptier, the passersby quieter, and the eyes I could feel watching me were less friendly than they'd been yesterday. Maybe I was imagining things that weren't there, me being me, but I felt like the people today were almost *hostile.*

And if they were, I was pretty sure I knew why. Yesterday, I'd just arrived, so they'd been happy to see me, full of hope that I'd fix everything. Today, I was still here, but nothing had been fixed.

In fact, things were worse. The little canals around the Artists' Quarter were almost empty.

Which meant the Old Well was almost empty.

You're not doing enough, my brain said. *This is your fault.*

I reminded myself that my brain told lies all the time.

But it also sometimes told the truth.

Which was this?

"Well?" came the sound of Natasha's voice behind

me. I turned to see that she had winked into existence on the library steps and was standing with her hands on her hips, looking at us like *we* were the ones keeping *her* waiting. "Do you want me to cast this spell or not?"

"Good morning, Natasha," Pip said in an exaggeratedly merry voice, swooping around her head in circles that I suspected he intended to be annoying. "What a pleasure it is to see you."

"Of course it is," she said. "I am me."

"You are," he replied. "Remind me again, what do the other witches call you? Saint Natasha, Her Epic Majesty? That's it. Because of how saintly and epic you are."

"*Saintly* is a stretch," she said modestly. "I am quite certain I have faults. Two, at most."

Suki made a choked sound that was undoubtedly a giggle.

Tugging on one of Pip's tail feathers in warning, I started up the steps before Lej strangled Natasha or Natasha strangled Pip, neither of which would help us rescue Kaveri and break the curse.

As we reached the threshold of the library, Numa, the gargoyle, marched out to plant himself in front of us.

He took one look at Simha, stuck his nose higher in the air, and said, "No. I will not allow *him* into the Ancient Library."

"You don't own the Ancient Library, Numa," Simha said, tossing his big head. "It is public property. I can come in if I wish."

"I hate you," said the gargoyle.

"I hated you first," Simha retorted.

"You are both too old to behave in such an undignified manner," Natasha said, looking like she was deeply regretting her generosity in offering to come here today. "Numa, I am in need of an object you keep in the restricted and highly unsafe section."

I wondered why she kept persisting in calling it by such an absurd name, but then I noticed a small sign on one of the library walls: an arrow pointing to the left with the words RESTRICTED AND HIGHLY UNSAFE under it. Oh. It was *actually* called the Restricted and Highly Unsafe section.

Numa gave Natasha a deeply suspicious look. "Which object?"

"A fragment of antler belonging to the demon Sura."

"Why?"

"Why are you so interested in my business?"

"You, you, you," Numa said scathingly. "Everything isn't about *you*."

"Then who is it about?" Natasha demanded, looking so offended that I had to smother a laugh. When Numa just rolled his eyes at her, she pointed a finger at him. "Answer me, gargoyle, before I turn you back to the rock from whence you came."

Simha looked like he'd never been happier.

I sighed. "You're not exactly subtle, are you?" I asked Natasha.

"I work best unsubtly. My sisters used to call me a blunt instrument."

"I don't think they were referring to your interrogation approach," Numa remarked.

The Good Witch turned to me, her expression demanding enlightenment.

I bit my lip. "Um, *blunt* is also the opposite of *sharp*. Numa's suggesting that your sisters were saying you're not sharp."

"Oh." Natasha sniffed contemptuously. "He thinks I'm stupid. I see."

"I doubt that," said Numa.

Suki succumbed to an alarming fit of coughing.

"Numa," I said quickly. "We don't want to take the antler fragment out of the library, and we won't damage it in any way. We just need the Good Witch to cast a tracking spell on it so that we can find Sura. Please?"

Simha grumbled, "We do not need his permission. Public. Property."

Numa's gray face turned purple. "Ugly. Lion."

"*How dare you?*" Simha roared.

"That's enough!" I said very loudly and very sternly. "Both of you can quit it right this minute. Are we understood?"

They objected. "He started—"

"Are we understood?"

Looking slightly ashamed of themselves, Simha and Numa nodded.

"The antler, if you please," said Natasha.

Numa jerked his head to the left. "This way."

The Restricted and Highly Unsafe section of the Ancient Library was much like the rest of the library, with plenty of shelves of old books and dusty paintings on the walls, but there was one exception: there were a whole lot of *other* things in the room, too. Statues of gods and gargoyles, a number of cracked and broken vases and vessels, a rusty pair of swords, and a whole shelf of smaller, weirder artifacts.

"Why is this section unsafe?" I asked curiously.

Numa didn't hesitate. "Because I will murder you if you get so much as a scratch on a single object," he said. "Do not touch anything."

Seemingly unable to help himself, Simha lifted a paw very slowly and deliberately and touched the tip of his claw to the gilded frame of a painting. Numa ground his teeth but said nothing, possibly because Natasha was already at his side and reaching for a pale, dusty object on a shelf. With his bony arms crossed tightly over his tweed jacket, he watched her like a hawk, obviously ready to pounce the instant she so much as *breathed* wrong.

I stepped closer to look at the fragment of antler in Natasha's hands. It just looked like a pale sliver of bone, so ordinary and unthreatening. I couldn't believe it had come from Sura.

"If you don't mind," Natasha said, and I could tell she was using her Wise and Mysterious Witch Voice, probably for Numa's benefit. "I need space to summon the song of the fireflies."

I rolled my eyes. So did Numa. We both stepped away from her. I turned just in time to see Samara clap her hands over her mouth.

"What's wrong?"

"That *book,*" she breathed, gazing at a big dusty tome lying propped open on a sturdy wooden easel. "That's the Beast Book."

"The what?"

"That is *not* what it's called," Numa scoffed. "That book is *The True and Complete History of the Heavenly Beasts.*"

"Nicknamed the Beast Book," said Samara. Her eyes were bright with excitement and wonder, and she didn't seem to be able to tear them away from the book. "I thought it didn't exist. It's supposed to be the oldest record of the most ancient beasts and creatures that came from the heavens, many of which are long gone now."

I had a feeling I knew what the answer was going to be, but I couldn't help saying hopefully, "Numa, I don't suppose we could—"

"Absolutely not," said the gargoyle. "That book stays where it is. There is a reason it's in the Restricted and Highly Unsafe section, you know. It is far too precious for me to allow it to be tarnished by the grubby fingers of children."

I thought fast, dredging up what I could from my mother's and grandparents' stories. "But it probably has all kinds of information about old mysterious creatures, like the Naga king who could control the weather," I said. "Doesn't Sura's curse sound like something that controls the weather? What if there's a clue in there that helps us break the curse?"

"No," said Numa, unmoved.

For the first time, I actually *hoped* Simha would intervene, but it seemed he, like the others, hadn't noticed our conversation because he was more interested in watching Natasha cast her spell than in an old dusty book. Which was totally fair.

But it was a *really* cool book.

Samara gave me a rueful smile. "You get it, don't you?"

"I do," I said mournfully. "I really do."

"Look!" Suki squealed. "It's happening!"

I turned back to see that the fragment of Sura's antler

had started to glow. It wasn't in Natasha's hands anymore; it hovered a few inches above her right palm while her left hand drew shapes in the air around it. The sliver of antler glowed brighter and brighter, forcing us all to shield our eyes.

When the light faded, the antler sliver looked completely ordinary again. It dropped into Natasha's palm, and she put it back on the shelf.

"Did it work?" Pip asked doubtfully.

Natasha threw him an affronted look. "Of course it worked." She held up her left hand, which she'd closed into a fist, and opened it to show us something that looked like a small bright feather made out of the same glowy light that had engulfed the antler fragment. As soon as her hand opened, the feather of light started moving, like it was going to drift or fly away, but she snatched it out of the air again and gestured imperiously at us. "An empty vessel, if you please."

We glanced at each other. "What kind of vessel?"

"Any."

"You could have mentioned that yesterday," Lej said irritably. "We didn't bring anything."

"I have a locket," Suki said doubtfully. She took her necklace off and opened the round locket that had been hanging from it. Inside was a small piece of knitted yellow cloth, which she tucked carefully into a pocket of her jeans before handing the locket over to the Good Witch. At my curious look, she said, "It's all that's left of a blanket our father made us when we were babies. The blanket burned with everything else in the fire that killed our parents, uncle, and grandmother."

My heart hurt. "I'm sorry." It wasn't just the *I'm sorry* of sympathy. It was *I'm sorry because I did that to you.* It was *I'm sorry because I decided a crew of rebel orphans was a fun idea and I didn't know a monster would make you real.*

I loved the Crows too much to regret that they were real, and I knew Mahishasura's magic had done most of the storytelling, but I wished for the thousandth time that I hadn't been so keen on the stupid orphan idea. I didn't often miss having a father, mostly because I'd never known what it was like to have one in the first place and I had Mum, but it must have been in the back of my mind when I was creating my sketchbook world.

Natasha cleared her throat pointedly. Once she had my attention, she sealed the little feather of light into Suki's locket. "When you have made your preparations and are ready to face Sura," she said, "release the feather and it will lead you to her."

Suki took the locket back. As soon as it was out of her hands, Natasha winked out of existence.

"Not even a goodbye," Numa, who was not exactly the prince of good manners, grumbled.

Simha grunted, which was apparently the only way he would allow himself to show that he actually agreed with his archnemesis. "Well," he rumbled, turning to me, "I suppose we should—"

Suki made an odd noise.

"You okay?" I asked her.

She was looking around the room. "Where's Samara?"

The rest of us looked. Pip even checked behind Simha to see if she'd decided to play the most weirdly timed game of hide-and-seek ever, but she was nowhere to be found.

At first, this was just puzzling, because it wasn't like Samara to just wander off and not tell anyone where she was going. On the other hand, we *were* in a library, and Samara behaved in very un-Samara-like ways in libraries.

But then I looked over at the sturdy wooden easel, and my heart dropped to my shoes.

The Beast Book, which had been lying open and dusty the last time I'd seen it, was now firmly shut.

14

"Oh, she *didn't*," I sighed.

Suki groaned. "Please tell me she hasn't gone and gotten herself gobbled up by another book!"

"I think she has."

Numa's enormous eyes bulged. "She touched the Beast Book?"

I took it as a sign of how badly Numa was taking this news that he had stooped to using the book's nickname.

"You can get her out, can't you?" I asked.

He gave me a sour look. "I'm not sure I should bother, given I did very specifically warn you all not to touch any—"

Simha growled so loudly that we had to put our hands over our ears to try to block it out.

"Oh, shut up, you overprotective cat," Numa said grumpily. "Of course I'll get her out. I can't have clumsy children living inside precious and dangerous artifacts!"

"He's more concerned about the book than about Samara, isn't he?" Pip said in my ear.

"It does sound like it."

"I will get her out," Numa repeated. "But it will take some time."

Suki was starting to look worried. "How much time?"

"If you're lucky, she'll be out by tomorrow."

"It's going to take a whole *day* to get her out? Will she be okay?"

"Why wouldn't she be?" Numa asked. "It's a book, not a viper. She is most likely having a marvelous time wandering around among the words as we speak. As long as she's out in a day or two, I suspect she'll suffer no ill effects other than dehydration. A complaint we shall *all* soon be suffering from," he added pointedly, "if you don't go break that curse like you keep saying you will."

The Crows, Simha, and I looked at each other. "We can't just leave her," I protested.

"I do not like it, either," said Simha.

"I don't think we have much of a choice," said Lej

grimly. His fists were clenched, and I knew he wasn't happy about it, but he was also nothing if not practical. "We *could* plant ourselves right here and do absolutely nothing until tomorrow, but do you really think that's the best use of our time?"

I remembered the hostile expressions on people's faces and thought of how little water had been in the canals outside. I *hated* when Lej was right, but I also knew he was.

Still—

"Suki?" I asked. "What do *you* want to do?"

Suki's lip wobbled, but she closed her hand tightly around her locket and said, "I think we should go find Sura. If Numa's right, Samara will be okay inside the book until he can get her out. She wouldn't want us to wait here and waste time."

"Do you want to stay while the rest of us take the locket and go?"

"You might need me," she replied, and that was that.

So we left, reluctantly. Simha bounded off to the Summer Palace to summon Chamundeshwari, and the rest of us went back to Crow House, where we explained everything to Jojo and a disinterested Joy over a hasty, half-hearted lunch.

I, for one, could barely eat. The part I'd been dreading was here at last.

It's okay, I said to myself. *Eyes straight ahead, remember? You know what to do. Find the powerful Asura, stop the powerful Asura, rescue the princess, conquer the curse, and save the kingdom.*

Easy peasy, said my brain sarcastically.

Getting ready to go was easy, at least. Suki went out to the greenhouse I'd made her to gather as many useful plants, herbs, and potions as she could think of. Lej clipped his folded metal wings over his shoulders, threading them through slits in his jacket, and then went to retrieve his sword, Jojo's bow, and a knife for me. ("*Just* so you can defend yourself," he said, probably vividly remembering how it had gone the last time someone had put a pointy weapon in my hands.)

Pip had a few of his old mayhem-making devices in his room, so he got Lej to help him retrieve the ones he couldn't carry in either his beak or his talons. None of us wore the superhero-esque costumes we'd worn when we fought Mahishasura, maybe because none of us could bear to when Ashwini, Pip, and Samara couldn't, but Jojo made sure we were all wearing pieces of armor he'd designed: coats with stardust stitching so that they would repel claws and steel, hiking boots that made no sound when we moved, and bracelets that meant no transformation or illusion spells would work on us.

All that was left to figure out was how we were going to travel, and that part was up to me.

It was a pretty safe bet that Sura was in the Magicwood, but the forest was enormous, sprawling over hills and valleys, and there was no way we would be able to cover those kinds of distances on foot with any kind of speed. In India, when we'd gone to Gramps's family's coffee farm and passed through the huge forest that had inspired the Magicwood, we'd gone in a big rumbling Jeep, but I didn't have time to figure out how to draw a working one to life. The train and the red bus, the only two modern-ish transports in the Kikiverse, had both been created when I'd just been putting doodles down in my sketchbook and I hadn't been the one to bring them to life.

I had to pick something simpler. When we'd marched on Lalith Mahal to confront Mahishasura, I'd created a mechanical chariot for Jojo and Natasha, which Natasha had taken after the battle and stashed who knows where. It would have been too small for all of us anyway, but it was the right idea. A chariot pulled by a pair of clockwork horses would let us cross big distances quickly. And I could draw it to life in an hour.

I checked my phone, but I'd only had it since my birthday the month before, so I hadn't had time to download the hordes of reference pictures I had on my clunky old laptop at home. I knew what a horse basically looked like, of course, but I didn't want to risk *creating* one without at least one or two reference pictures.

Gathering up my pencil and the scrap materials Lej had given me from his scavenger stash, I went upstairs to the library I'd made for Samara. It felt weird being in there without her, but it was a lovely, cozy room, and Samara kept it so orderly that it took me only a minute to find a book with sketches and paintings of horses in it.

Pip flew in just as I started sketching shapes onto pieces of scrap metal and wood. I looked up at him, and for just a moment, as the sunlight hit him, it was like his crow form vanished and the golden silhouette of a boy took its place.

A blink, and the illusion was gone. Our eyes met.

"Do you remember it?" I asked.

Pip cocked his head. "Dying? No. One minute I was in Mahishasura's fortress, and then the next I was a crow. I was lucky, I guess. *You* had to live through it, but I didn't. I got to miss out on the bad stuff."

"I don't think I lived through it, either," I admitted. "So much was happening so fast that there wasn't time to properly *feel* it, and then you came back and I didn't have to."

"But you watched me die, and that did something to you. I know you dream about it. You talk in your sleep."

I tightened my grip on my pencil. "Every time I worry about Lej and his wings or Samara inside that book, I think about what Mahishasura did to you."

"You're afraid of all those terrible feelings you never had to feel because I came back," Pip guessed. "You're afraid that, like Sura's curse, you're only holding them at bay until—"

He stopped, but I finished it for him, a lump in my throat: "Until you go for good."

"Why would I go?"

"Because ghosts don't stay forever!"

Pip made a scoffing sound deep in his feathered throat. "Wanna bet?"

I laughed, but I wondered if Pip *wanted* to go. Had he left somewhere warm and peaceful just to come back? Was there a light calling him? I had no idea what happened after people died, in either universe, but for all I knew, maybe Pip didn't *want* to be here.

"Don't stay just for me," I said quickly. "If you want to go, you should. You don't have to stay just because I need you."

"That's very noble of you, Kiki," Pip applauded. "I'll keep that in mind the next time your snoring keeps me up all night."

"I don't snore!"

Laughing, he flew out of the room, putting an end to the conversation. I went back to the chariot and horses, trying to refocus. As my pencil moved, I pictured the way I wanted my creations to look, and they reshaped themselves into three-dimensional legs, heads, and panels until, at last, there was a mechanical chariot and two moving, snorting mechanical horses on the floor of Samara's library.

"Those horses are too small," said a sorrowful voice

from the doorway. I looked up at Joy, disoriented as always by the way he looked out of focus. "I knew I'd bring you bad luck. I did warn you, didn't I? You shouldn't have taken me in. Everything I touch turns to—"

"Don't start that," I said hastily.

The chariot and horses *were* small, about the right size for a doll to ride, but they were *supposed* to be small. It made it very easy for me to carry them downstairs, round up the others, and go outside.

The afternoon sun had warmed the air, so it was a lot less cold than it had been this morning, and the coats Jojo had given us to wear were almost too hot for the weather. Simha had already returned with Chamundeshwari, who had swapped her white toga and unbound hair for her old braid and armored tunic.

I put the chariot and horses down on the cobblestones. Pip immediately dropped to the ground to make friends with the snorting, prancing miniature clockwork horses.

"Whenever you're ready," I said to Suki, who had seemed like a TV on mute since we'd left the Ancient Library, her noisy exuberance decidedly less noisy and exuberant without her twin sister beside her.

Perking up, she reached for the wand and witch's spellbook she'd brought outside with her. When I'd drawn the hundreds of tin toy soldiers we'd used to trick Mahishasura into thinking we had an army, Natasha had performed a resizing spell on them. At some point after the battle, the twins had somehow browbeaten her into adding the spell to the Crows' spellbook, which meant Suki could now cast it.

"Step back," she warned us.

An instant later, the white clockwork horses were even bigger than actual horses, and the sturdy, sleek wood-and-metal chariot was no longer a toy. I couldn't help admiring my own handiwork as we started packing in our gear and other supplies. I'd created a high, comfortable perch at the rear of the chariot for Jojo, who would need some height to fire arrows from if we met something unfriendly. In front of the perch, tucked low so that no one's head would get in Jojo's way, were three rows of cozy, cushioned benches with plenty of room for the rest of us. Including Simha, if he decided he wanted a break from running.

Lej and Suki started fighting over who would get to steer the horses first. When Chamundeshwari pointed out that she was only one who had actually driven a chariot into battle before and that *she* should therefore probably steer first, Lej and Suki argued over who would get to drive after Chamundeshwari had her turn. Suki won by shamelessly brandishing the “my sister is trapped in a book and I’m very upset” card, Joy wondered out loud if his own sorrows meant *he* got to have a turn, too, and the rest of us simply piled in so that we could get moving before the Old Well went completely dry.

“Okay, Suki,” I said, and she opened up her locket.

The small, bright, glowing feather flew out of the locket. It was so tiny, but it was unmistakable even in the sunlight. It hovered in front of the chariot for an instant and then darted away.

Chamundeshwari flicked the reins, there was a whir and click of clockwork, and the horses took off into the dimming golden light of the day.

15

We shot across the city, even faster than the train. The feather of light led us northeast to the Magicwood, just as we'd expected.

I looked up into the sky, past the pale-pink castle in the clouds. The sun would be gone in a couple of hours. That hadn't bothered me last night, or the night before, but I'd been in the city then, in parts of the Kikiverse I knew. Tonight would be different. I'd dreamed up the Magicwood, but only the idea of it. I didn't know it the way I knew the city. I didn't know what was waiting for us inside it.

I wasn't afraid of the dark, but the dark *did* make it a little too easy for my brain to conjure up monsters in every shadow, and I had a feeling that was going to be even easier in a mysterious, enchanted forest where I knew there *would* be monsters.

And while I was thinking of mysterious things, what about the tiny golden triangle tattoo on my wrist? Pip didn't have one, but the other Crows and I did. Who had put them on us? Why? What if—

Nope. Nope. Nope. No spiraling. Not now. I had to save it for—

Oh.

It hit me then that I hadn't actually allowed myself my thirty minutes of worry time in days. Two evenings ago, I'd been too busy trying to keep Mum from finding out why Lej had really come to London, and then, of course, we'd come here. And last night, after getting back to Crow House after talking to the Asura general, there had been so much to talk about with the others that I'd forgotten all about it.

It was no wonder my brain had been getting noisier and noisier since I'd come back to the Kikiverse. I'd thought it was because there was a lot to worry about, but it wasn't just that.

Remembering Dr. Muzembe telling me to ground

myself, I started listing things. I could see my dreamy, impractical, childish castle in the sky. I could see Pip flying above us, swooping this way and that, his boy cries mingling with crow caws. I could smell dry leaves and jasmine. I could feel the difference in the texture of my skin where I must have scraped my palm on the rocks at the edge of Lake Lune. I could see people watching us as the horses galloped past. I could feel Lej's elbow beside me. I could see Simha running beside the chariot, his huge, powerful legs pounding into the cobblestones.

By the time I was firmly back in the here and now, Suki was driving the chariot, whooping gleefully as she followed Chamundeshwari's gentle instructions. On one side of me, Lej's eyes were alert. *Gogglers peeled*, as Ashwini used to tell them. On my other side, Joy watched the city fly past us, looking mournful and a little wistful.

"Do you remember much of your life from before?" I asked the ghost. It seemed as good a time as any to try to find out what his unfinished business might be.

Joy gave a shrug. "I remember enough that I wish I did not. I told you, everything I touch turns to—"

"Ash and ruin and all that," I said quickly. "Yes, you've said. Why is that?"

"Poor choices, for the most part," he said morosely. "I was also bespelled, but I cannot blame my ruinous nature on that."

I was so surprised, I turned my whole body on the bench to look at him. Well, I tried, anyway. It was extremely peculiar to be right beside him and to still find myself unable to get a proper look at him. It felt like the time I'd tried on Gramps's reading glasses and everything had looked out of focus.

"Someone put a spell on you?" I asked him. A thought struck me. "Was it the Good Witch? Is that why you were on the rocks outside the lighthouse when we found you?"

"I think the spell is why I am here, neither alive nor dead," said Joy. "I cannot be certain. That part is foggy. It was intended to be a punishment, I think, for my monstrousness."

This sounded very dramatic to me, but I was hardly one to talk. "Joy, we're on our way to find a demon whose curse will literally destroy everyone and everything in this universe if we can't break it," I said, trying to make him feel better. "Now, *that's* monstrous."

"Monsters come in many forms."

"So do heroes," Chamundeshwari offered from the

bench in front of us. "Kiki and I are very different, but we have both been heroic. Who is to say you cannot be, too?"

"*I* say," said Joy. "Everything I touch turns to—"

"Make him stop or I'll push him out of the chariot," Lej growled at me.

I decided it was probably best to give up on helping Joy finish his unfinished business. At least for now.

The feather of light had led us out of the city. It wasn't long before we were approaching the wide, long bridge that had once arched over the Kaveri, connecting the city and the Magicwood on either side of the river. Now the river was gone and the bridge was a shadowy, smoky blur across the Void.

I felt cold, and it wasn't just because of the Void. It was because this was the bridge where we had stood and scattered Pip's ashes.

Something warm settled against my neck. Pip had landed on my shoulder. I wondered if he was thinking of it, too.

Then Simha let out a low snarl of warning, effectively chasing every other thought out of my mind. Looking past Suki, Chamundeshwari, and the horses, I saw what he'd seen.

In the distance, halfway down the bridge and half-hidden by the shadows of the Void, something glowed. A *lot* of somethings.

A lot of snarling, crystalline somethings.

I gulped.

"You see?" Joy gestured with a gloomy kind of satisfaction. "Ruin. I warned you."

"You had nothing to do with this, so pipe down," I said. "Those are Sura's creatures."

Behind us, Jojo already had his bow in his hands. I had no idea how he was going to aim with the chariot jolting unevenly across the stone of the bridge, but I knew he knew what he was doing, and I trusted him to do it. Meanwhile, with Pip still on my shoulder, I scrambled over the back of the front bench to squeeze in beside Suki.

"Should we just drive the horses straight at them?" she asked me, panicking.

After drawing her sword with an earsplitting shriek of steel, Chamundeshwari put a bracing hand on my shoulder. "Do not stop. Do not slow down. The tracking spell will not wait for you, so you must keep following it. Simha and I will hold off the beasts."

She rose to her feet, strong and sure, and sprang

straight from the moving chariot to Simha's back. Suki let out a squeak, her hands clutching the reins so tightly that her knuckles were white. I put my hands over hers to help her keep the horses steady.

With a roar that shook the earth, lion and goddess charged into battle.

16

Simha slammed into the waiting phalanx of beasts, breaking one into a thousand bright pieces and scattering the others. They let out unearthly howls, the same sounds coming eerily out of all the beasts' mouths as if they had only a single voice between them, and they flung themselves at him. Chamundeshwari's sword flashed as she struck.

The horses kept going, galloping closer and closer to the battle on the bridge. Real horses probably would have shied away or sent us all tumbling off the bridge in terror, but these were clockwork horses, and they had no more awareness of what was in front of them than a car would.

I didn't dare look back at the others. My hands were still on Suki's, keeping the horses steady, and my heart was thundering in my chest in time with their hooves. An arrow shot past us from the perch, narrowly missing one of the beasts, and then Simha roared, swept out one of his enormous paws, and knocked several snarling, glowing creatures out of our way.

With a path cleared for us, we drove right through the battle and down the bridge.

"Look out!" Pip shouted, smacking one wing across the side of my face as if it could somehow shield me.

A lithe cat-creature, identical to the one that had attacked me at the Void the night before last, had tried to spring into the chariot beside me (Was it the *same* one? Did these creatures have some way of putting themselves back together?), but Pip's talons went straight for its eyes, and then Lej knocked it away with the blunt end of his sword.

I looked back just once to see Simha and Chamundeshwari surrounded by glowing beasts and shattered shards of light. Then the shadows of the Void made it impossible to see them anymore, the chariot raced ahead, and we plunged into the Magicwood.

"Where's the ghost?" Lej yelled.

"He vanished right after Chamundeshwari left," Pip told him. "Just poof! Gone! I think he was scared."

"We're *all* scared!"

"Keep going!" Jojo shouted over the others' voices. "We're being followed!"

Beside me, Suki was shaking. I was, too, but I let the words *Eyes straight ahead, Kiki* repeat themselves over and over in my mind as I took the reins from her. I just hoped I could keep the horses from crashing into a tree.

There was no road or path in the forest, just spaces between the towering trees dappled by long shadows and the last of the sunlight. I aimed for the spaces and followed the glowing feather darting merrily ahead of us, but it was almost impossible to keep from colliding into *something*. I wasn't sure what would be worse: hitting a tree, or slowing down and letting one of Sura's beasts catch up.

"They're falling back," Jojo called out. "Don't slow down yet, but I think we might have almost outrun them."

My romper and coat were both stuck to my skin, my

back and armpits soaked in ice-cold sweat. It felt horrid, but that was almost a good thing because it was something to think about that wasn't *What if we crash what if the beasts catch up what if something happens to the Crows what if we can't save the city what will Mum do if I don't ever go home—*

I lost track of the seconds, then the minutes. My brain rebelled, running down dark paths, but I kept dragging it back to the cold sweat under my arms, the sound of my heart in my ears. My eyes were raw from staring almost unblinking at the feather and trees in front of the horses. My hands were numb with cold and aching from holding the reins so tightly for so long. These were the things I needed to think about, the things I had to pay careful attention to so that there was no space to think about all those horrible what-ifs.

It was dark by the time Jojo said he was pretty sure we'd lost the creatures. The sounds of owls and other birds trilling happily in the trees seemed to confirm that, but Pip flew up high to double-check and swooped back triumphantly. "Not a glowing beastie in sight," he informed us.

"Kiki." Suki, who was huddled beside me, put a cold hand on my arm. "Let Lej drive. You need to take a break."

I nodded shakily and slowed the horses so that I could trade places with Lej. We didn't stop for even a moment, but Lej kept us going at a slower pace, weaving more cautiously through the much darker spaces between the trees. Here, where the Magicwood was deep, very little moonlight filtered in, and it wasn't easy to see anything other than the horses and the shining feather.

Back on the middle bench, I allowed myself a minute or two to catch my breath and feel a *little* less like my heart was about to explode right out of me. Then I pulled one of my pencils out of my romper pocket.

"Lanterns," I explained, drawing half a dozen of them to life. They bathed the chariot in a pool of golden light, chasing away some of the shadows. "When we stop, I'll draw a Rudolph nose on the horses, too. I should have thought of that before we left."

"A *what* nose?" Suki asked, twisting around to look at me.

It was as good a distraction as any, so I told them

about Rudolph the Red-Nosed Reindeer, which then led to telling them about Santa Claus, and when *that* was done, Suki and Jojo told me some of their own stories. And so it went, story after story to chase the dark and the monsters away.

Everything had been peaceful for almost an hour when, with a pop, Joy materialized on the bench beside me. I yelped.

"You're back!" said Pip. "Where'd you go?"

"Away," said Joy, shuddering. "I was overcome by fear, and I abandoned you. Judge me if you must, but you cannot make me anything other than what I am."

Lej scowled at him. "Which is what, exactly? A coward?"

"I am indeed cowardly," said the ghost, nodding glumly. "I always have been. I have but the slimmest of backbones. Put me in peril, and without fail, I will experience the greatest panic. One time, I saw a frog and—"

"It's okay," Pip said merrily.

"No, it isn't," said Joy. "I abandoned you. It is only right that you spurn me!"

"Fine, you're spurned," said Jojo. "Feel better?"

Joy sighed. "Never."

Pip started to laugh. Then the rest of us were laughing, too. Even Lej. It might have just been a delayed reaction to outrunning an army of unearthly beasts, but the next thing we knew, we were all doubled over, tears in our eyes, laughing so hard it hurt in the best way.

"Stop, stop," Lej begged as the chariot wobbled. "I can't steer like this."

"You are all very peculiar," said Joy, mystified.

That just made the rest of us laugh even harder.

Unfairly, the laughter was what got us. If we hadn't been laughing so hard, we might have noticed that the birds in the trees had gone quiet. If we hadn't been clutching our sides and wiping tears from our eyes, we might have noticed that the feather of light was no longer the only thing glowing in the deep dark of the Magicwood.

But we didn't notice until it was too late, so when the beasts came out of the trees on either side of the chariot, it was a surprise.

Pip let out a shrill crow screech and Lej jerked the reins, but it was too late. As the air around us turned frosty with cold, the beasts pounced. One horse toppled over, the chariot skewed violently sideways, and there was a terrible, thunderous crash.

The world spun. I hit something hard and landed on my back. I saw leaves, a glimpse of a night sky, and then nothing.

17

The lost, angry girl in the dark was watching me. She had a name, and I knew that I knew it, but I had a terrible headache and I couldn't seem to remember it.

"I am not bound to the earth you walk upon, world-builder," she said. Once again, I felt like I was choking on grief, rage, and fear, but none of them were mine. "You will not find me."

"I will," I said. I wasn't sure why, but I knew I had to. "I promise. I'll find you."

I blinked, and she was gone. There was a dull ringing in my ears, and stars wheeled above me. One blink, then another, and it started to come back to me. The Magicwood. The chase. Cold sweat. Laughing. The creatures pouncing. The crash of the chariot.

I was still on my back. My breath was frost in front of me. Someone had me by the shoulders. Her red leather jacket caught the light.

"Why are *you* here?" I rasped, pushing her away. "You betrayed us. You don't get to be here now."

"You're alive," the girl in the red leather jacket said. "Good. The others need you."

I blinked, and then Ashwini was gone, too. My head throbbed. How many lost girls were waiting for me in the shadows?

I tried to get up, but my head started to spin and I fell back. I rolled over instead and crawled. I was at the foot of a huge, hulking tree, where I must have landed when the chariot crashed and overturned, and I could hear the others close by.

I crawled around the tree. There was someone else on the other side of it. Jojo. He was silent and still, but—*Is he breathing is he breathing yes yes he's breathing he's okay stop it Kiki eyes straight ahead.* Jojo was unconscious, and his chair was overturned in the grass a few feet away. Out of reach.

Jojo and I weren't alone. Suki stood in front of us, her back to us, and beyond her was a ring of beasts. The beasts had us trapped, but Suki, tiny Suki, was fighting anyway. She was a whirlwind of light and colors as she flung orbs and spells at the beasts, freezing them in place, sending them flying backward, even *melting* them. My brain, still aching and sluggish, struggled to keep up. Joy was nowhere to be seen, but there was Pip, a winged black shadow diving at the beasts, screeching, talons out.

And then something impossible came out of the sky, enormous wings spread wide. A winged man with a sword. An archangel? Wasn't that what winged men with swords usually were? He slammed into the beasts from above, distracting them, luring them away from the rest of us and then striking them down.

No, I thought, as my brain caught up at last. *Not an angel. A boy with metal wings.*

"Worldbuilder," the beasts snarled in sync, in one cold voice. Sura's voice. "Cursebreaker. You will fail."

You will fail. The words that dogged me, no matter what I did. Did Sura lie, the way my brain so often did?

"You should have left this universe while you still could," she went on, her voice coming from everywhere at once. "This is not your war, and I will not let you interfere."

The beasts weren't stopping. Even as they shattered, they were putting themselves back together. Even as they melted, they were reforming into wolves and lynxes and jackals. It didn't matter how many of them Suki threw potions at, how many Pip and Lej struck from above. They kept coming back.

And the feather—

My heart plummeted. The feather of light was gone.

Even if we survived the beasts, how would we find Sura? How would we rescue Kaveri and save the Kiki-verse?

You will fail.

Unless—

I wobbled, but I gritted my teeth. I could do this. I could. I squeezed Jojo's hand, hoping he would wake up soon, hoping he was okay, and then staggered to my feet.

"Stop!" I shouted, my voice cracking. *"Stop!"*

Suki almost dropped her wand. The others turned, shocked.

But the beasts went still.

I looked from one beast to the next. "I'm the one who

interfered," I said to the demon watching me through their eyes. "I'm the one who can break the curse. Curse-breaker. That's what you called me. So you can have me. Just let the others go."

There was an uproar. Suki looked like she wanted to shake me. Lej snapped at me. "Kiki, don't you *dare*—"

"This is the only way," I said to them. I looked at each of their faces, lingering on Pip's the longest, willing them to understand. "Sura's beasts will take me to her, and no one will meddle with her curse, and the rest of you will be okay."

"But . . ." Suki's lip trembled.

"Let me do this," I said to the Crows, and to the beasts.

The beasts cocked their heads at me, all eerily, creepily in sync. "What if I choose to kill you once I have you?" they asked me.

"I'd really prefer it if you didn't," I croaked. "You don't have to hurt me. You could just keep me out of the way until your curse has done what it's supposed to. Then you can send me home. And the Crows could come with me, too. If they're safe, it won't matter what happens to the rest of the kingdom."

"Wait, what?" Suki whispered, confused, but Lej grabbed her hand to shush her.

"Intriguing," the beasts mused. "You brought ruin down on Mahishasura when he threatened this world, yet you'd abandon it now?"

"I fought him for *them*," I said, pointing at the Crows. "If you let them go, I won't get in your way. You can keep me to make sure of it."

There was nothing at all false about my fear. I was *terrified*. I was a small, frightened girl who wished she had a fierce lion or a warrior goddess or even just her mother here to keep her safe. Every one of the beasts could probably hear it in my heartbeat, see it in the shaky bob of my throat.

I'd used my very real fear to trick Mahishasura. Maybe, just maybe, I could use it to trick Sura, too.

Because this wasn't *just* about protecting the Crows. With the Old Well drying up and the tracking spell way out of reach, there was only one way to find Sura.

Her beasts had to take me to her.

"Very well," said the beasts, cold and amused. "What difference do the lives of a few children make to me?

They may go. You, worldbuilder, will be my guest until we have seen the end of this kingdom."

I shuddered at the word *guest.* Pip let out a piteous caw but remained where he was, perched on Lej's shoulder.

"Will she be safe?" Suki demanded of the beasts. "Will you promise not to hurt her?"

"Would the promise of a monster be worth anything?" the beasts replied. A high laugh. "We will watch the end of the world together. You may choose to believe that or not."

I stepped away from the Crows, pushing my hands deep into the pockets of my coat to keep them warm. I didn't dare look back. I couldn't risk giving something away.

"You will want to ride," the beasts said to me. "We will be going a long way."

One of the two clockwork horses was still upright, a white ghost in the shadows of the Magicwood, snorting and tossing its head. Its reins were still keeping it tethered to the broken chariot, so I untied them and pulled myself up to sit on top of it.

"Try to keep up." The beasts laughed and took off into the forest.

I had ridden a horse exactly once in my entire life, at a classmate's tenth birthday party, and I had *not* enjoyed it. Not even a little bit. The horses themselves had been perfectly nice, but then I was on top of one and was so *high* off the ground and it was so *bumpy*, and now that I thought about it, that was probably around the time I'd first started worrying about things. More than people usually worry about things, I mean. I remembered that I'd mostly worried about getting thrown off the horse and breaking my neck. (Or worse, embarrassing myself in front of all my classmates!)

I pulled my mind back to the present: the cold night, the dark Magicwood, and the clockwork horse breaking into a sprint. I held on for dear life and ducked my head to avoid having branches hit me right in the face. Arms clenched around the horse's skeletal neck, I tried to count my breaths, in and out, in and out, to keep myself from spiraling into a panic.

I'd done what I'd hoped and was on my way to Sura, but now what? How would I rescue Kaveri by myself? All I had was my phone and a few pencils in the pocket of my romper, the pieces of armor Jojo had made me, and my uncooperative brain. Would they be enough?

You will fail. That wasn't Sura's voice this time. That was me, inside my own mind.

I kept track of how much time passed by measuring how much my tailbone hurt. A ridiculous bone, for a tail that wasn't even there.

Clockwork horses, it turned out, were *not* comfortable to ride.

We rode higher as the shapes of mountains peeked over the tops of the trees ahead, the angle of the ground tilting up. Abruptly, there was a broken gate and rows of trees on either side of what was unmistakably an overgrown road, and then, looming out of the dark, a tall cabin up on stilts.

It was a mess. It looked like the old hunting lodges I'd seen in India, with a long flight of rickety steps leading up to a sprawling wooden cabin elevated off the ground for a better view, but it was in worse shape than any of the other lodges I'd seen. The steps looked rotted, part of the roof was gone, and the balcony that surrounded the cabin was not much more than a few crooked planks. There were more of the crystalline beasts prowling the clearing, and oily lamplight spilled out of the few windows, so we had obviously come to the right place, but surely this couldn't be Sura's lair? Why would a powerful Asura live somewhere like this for over a hundred years?

I slid off the clockwork horse at the bottom of the steps, and my stiff, sore legs almost buckled under me. There were a million more important things to worry about, I knew that, and yet all I could think about was how mossy and rotten the wood of the steps looked and how undignified it would be if I were to tread on just the wrong spot, break the step, and plummet to my untimely demise. The Mughal emperor Humayun had died falling down the stairs, and that was pretty much all anyone ever remembered about *him*, so what chance did *I* have?

"Oh my god, stop it," I muttered. I was almost as bad as Joy! It was a grim thought.

I toed my way carefully up the long flight of stairs, one by one, wincing at every creak and groan of the wood. At the top, I felt a wonderful, heady rush of relief for exactly three seconds before I remembered that the steps had been the least of my problems.

Clenching my teeth to keep them from chattering, I went to the open doors of the lodge and stepped into the lit hall inside.

I saw her shadow first. It was exactly like the gandaberunda had shown me, a long, slender, antlered shadow stretching along the floor. My eyes followed the shadow all the way to the demon it belonged to.

For just one moment, the sight of an Asura sitting at the other end of the hall sent me right back to the memory of Mahishasura waiting for me on his throne. Panic immediately clutched at my throat, tightening its grip until I couldn't breathe.

Then I blinked, and the illusion was gone. They were nothing alike. Mahishasura had been sprawled haughtily in an opulent throne. Sura's throne was just a high-backed chair, and she sat stiffly in it. Mahishasura had surrounded himself with gold, jewels, and bones. Sura's lair was dusty, cobwebby, and rotten. I couldn't understand it.

"Come closer," she said imperiously, in the same high, cold voice the beasts had spoken to me with.

So she had *some* of Mahishasura's self-importance, then.

I crossed the hall until I was just a few steps away from her chair. Up close, I could see that she had two furred legs and cloven feet, like a faun, and two long, pale, viciously spiky antlers on top of her head. Her only hair was the same dull brown fur she had on her legs, the same fur that covered her human arms. Her torso was covered by a tattered brown dress. Her face was a deer's face, the nose and mouth extending outward, and her eyes had a glittering malice in them.

She looked cold and vengeful, but there was something *wrong* about the picture. She sat so stiffly in the chair. The *dusty* chair.

"So, worldbuilder," she said, "you have come to see the ruin."

I glanced around the high-ceilinged hall a little doubtfully, not certain *anyone* would want to come to see this. "The beasts," I said, summoning my voice. "How do you see and speak through them?"

"You may have noticed that they cannot be destroyed," she said, her mouth stretching into a smile I'd never seen on a deer. "They are tied to my life force. As long as I live, so do they. That link allows me to see with their eyes and speak with their jaws."

"So if you die, they . . ." I broke off, slightly horrified that I'd said it out loud.

Sura laughed. It was a mirthless, awful sound. "Are you thinking you might slay me, destroy my beasts, and break my curse all in one fell swoop, worldbuilder?" When my face grew hot, because that was of course *exactly* what I'd been thinking, she laughed again. "By all means, try. Do your very best to slay me. I give you my word, I will not lift a finger to stop you."

I found myself shaking my head. I'd buried Mahishasura under a palace, but the only reason I'd been able to do that was because he had murdered Pip and he had been savaging the city and *he* would have killed *me* if he had caught up to me. This was nothing like that.

"I don't want that, no matter what you've done," I said. "I just want to save the kingdom."

Her face darkened. "This kingdom was my ruin, worldbuilder. And now I will be *its* ruin."

It suddenly struck me that when she said, *You have come to see the ruin*, she hadn't meant the hunting lodge. She'd meant herself. *She* was the ruin.

"You could try your very best to kill me, and you would fail," she went on. "I cannot die."

"I know you're immortal, like Mahishasura and Chamundeshwari and every other creature from the heavens,"

I said, bewildered. "But that just means you *can* live forever, not that you *can't* be killed."

"You do not know what you speak of," she said coldly. "We can only die if our hearts are destroyed. Not broken, not stolen. *Destroyed.*"

Was that true? I thought of Ashwini in the bus in London, fighting the dragon Asura. The fight had been a show for my benefit, but the Asura *had* actually died. She'd struck him once, but his heart hadn't been where she'd expected it to be, so she had to strike him a second time to defeat him for good. She had to destroy his heart. And Mahishasura's heart had been crushed beneath the collapse of Mysore Palace.

"I don't understand," I said, feeling like I'd stumbled into a room halfway through a conversation and missed all the important bits. "Are you saying you can't be killed because your heart is not where it's supposed to be?"

"It was broken."

I stared. "Like, broken because of love?"

"Love?" She stared back at me contemptuously. "You do not know, do you? You are the architect of this world, yet you know nothing. A hundred and forty years ago, I came to this kingdom in friendship. It was not much of

anything then. Bountiful lands, but very little power and almost entirely ignored by the heavens. But its king, Mahindra, was ambitious."

"You and he fought," I said slowly. "Your grudge against the kingdom started with him."

"Mere pieces of the story. As I said, I came in friendship." Her eyes flashed. "Mahindra used my friendship to learn my secrets. He stole my heart as I slept, knowing I trusted him, and broke it. He thought it would give him my power, but the heavens' power cannot be used by a mortal. Out of spite, he tore my antler, banished me from the kingdom, and left me to die."

I swallowed. "That's not the story I was told."

"Stories are told by the winners, worldbuilder. That does not make them the truth."

I'd been told that before. When an admiral's statue had been torn down because important people had finally admitted that he had also owned slave ships. When I'd repeated something I was taught at school about the British Empire, and Mum had given me a long, sharp look and said, "That's not the version of the story your great-grandparents would have told you."

"What happened to you after that?" I asked quietly.

"My loyal companion brought me here, a place forgotten and far away," said Sura, gesturing beside her.

I took a startled step back. I hadn't even noticed the beast lying perfectly still next to the chair. Unlike Sura's other creatures, it was a real animal. A tiger, watchful, silent, and bony, its stripes faded, its eyes almost milky and blind with old age.

"I have not left since," Sura went on. "My grief turned to rage. I plotted. I spent decades gathering power for my curse. By the time I was ready, Mahindra's grandson Jai was on the throne."

"But *he* didn't do anything to you!" I protested. "The people of the city didn't do anything to you! Why did you curse everyone?"

"I offered to take back the curse," she said, "if Jai would return the heart Mahindra took from me. He pretended he knew nothing about it. So I stood by my curse."

"But all the *people*—"

"Is it my fault that the kings of this kingdom cared more for themselves than for their people?" Sura snarled. "You wish to make a monster out of me, worldbuilder, but know that I am not the only one in this tale. If my heart had been restored to me, all this would have ended."

I didn't know what to say. I'd come here expecting to find a monster, and I'd found one. Sura was willing to destroy an entire kingdom of people just to punish one person. That *was* monstrous. But she was right about how there were other monsters in this story, and looking at her now, sitting stiff and cold in that chair in the wreckage of this place, it was impossible not to see how much those other monsters had taken from her.

"If your heart is gone," I said softly, "does that mean you're trapped like this forever? Never able to die?"

"And never able to live, either," she said bitterly, and I thought of how peculiar it was that this entire quest had been punctuated by creatures who were neither alive nor dead. "I have been dying since the day my heart was taken and broken, but I cannot die. I have been weakened. My curse and my beasts are the only powers I still possess."

My thoughts stumbled over her words. "What you're saying can't be true. You *terrified* one of Mahishasura's generals. How did you do that if you have no power left?"

"A few of Mahishasura's minions have stumbled across

this lodge since they fled into the Magicwood," she acknowledged. "But they have great respect for me as an elder Asura and left as soon as they discovered it was I who dwelled here. I told them I would leave them in peace as long as they left me in peace. I did not frighten anyone."

"But—but—" None of this made sense. Sura could be lying, of course, but why bother lying about this? Yet nothing she had told me sounded like the Asura general's story of a terrifying, endless darkness and drowning on dry land and—

Wait. *Wait.*

Darkness. Drowning.

Something tugged at the edge of my thoughts, something I didn't want to look too closely at, but I looked anyway. My brain had never liked doing what I wanted it to.

I'd seen a lonely, endless dark place, and I'd seen the girl trapped there. I'd almost drowned, choking on ice-cold water that had come from an unnatural tempest. A tempest. Dark. Water. Water like the water Sura's curse had stolen, water like the water of a river.

"You . . ." My voice broke, and I had to try again. "She's not here, is she? You haven't imprisoned Kaveri."

"The princess who disrupted my curse?" Sura's

mouth twisted, an ugly and bitter line across her otherwise lovely deer face. "Tell me, worldbuilder: How could *I*, who have been dying for almost a century and a half, imprison a creature like that?"

Had I ever mentioned Sura's name to the Asura general? Had *he* ever mentioned the name of the monstrous creature that had frightened him so deeply? No matter how many times I turned the memory over and over in my mind, I couldn't remember a single name. Just that pronoun. *She*.

She, he'd said, and I'd assumed I knew who he meant. *She*, I'd said, and he'd assumed I was speaking of the same *she*.

The tempest on Lake Lune hadn't been the Good Witch casting a spell. The way she'd reacted to me accusing her of it, the way she'd repeated the words *my spell* and then said no more, I understood it now. She'd known there was no spell. She'd known what the tempest really was. And she'd lied to us.

A girl made of water, who could turn herself into a tempest, who could drown a demon on dry land. A monster who'd terrified the wits out of a fearsome general, a monster who'd almost killed Lej and me.

You will not find me, she'd said in the dark. It hadn't been a hopeless cry, as I'd thought. It had been a warning to an enemy.

I reeled. Sura had cursed the kingdom, but she hadn't done any of *this*.

Kaveri had.

Kaveri was the monster.

18

"It *can't* be."

The protest echoed in the high, ruined hall. I felt raw and betrayed.

I'd come here because of a story the Good Witch had told me, but she had lied. She'd let us come into the Magicwood, had *led* me to the den of a demon, knowing the whole time that the princess we wanted to rescue wasn't here.

I'd wanted to save Kaveri, but Kaveri didn't need saving. It was the rest of us who needed saving from her.

"You are distressed," Sura said curiously, her sharp eyes searching my face. "Why is that?"

"She wanted to save the kingdom," I said. "Didn't she?

Isn't that why she disrupted the curse? So why did she stop? Why did she try to drown me?"

Sura tapped the fingers of one hand against the arm of her chair. "If you weren't the most interesting thing to happen to me in decades, which is not saying much, I would not waste my time answering your childish questions," she remarked. I glared at her. "Once again, it seems you only have pieces of the story. Are you certain you want me to tell you the rest of it?"

No, I wasn't, but I had to know. I nodded.

"When I unleashed my curse on the kingdom, the rivers, lakes, and Old Well dried overnight. The rains stopped. There was panic, of course"—she said this with a certain amount of grim pleasure, and I shuddered—"and the people turned to King Jai, demanding he save them, demanding he act at once. He had none of his grandfather's charm, command, or intelligence, and he had no idea what to do. Then his daughter dreamed up an idea.

"'Papa,' she said. 'Let us ask a witch to turn *me* into a river for a short time. It may not break the curse, but it should surely interrupt it long enough for you to find and destroy this demon.'

"So the king and princess went to the witch, who

agreed to the scheme. She transformed the princess into a bottomless urn of water. They went to the empty riverbed and restored the river."

My stomach twisted. In Natasha's version of the story, Kaveri had never asked to be turned into a river for *a short time*. Natasha had made it sound like Kaveri had been willing to give up her human life for good.

"The people of your precious kingdom were delighted," Sura went on, her voice sharp with contempt. "They fell upon King Jai's feet, showering him with blessings and gratitude. They thought him a hero, forgetting all about the girl who had saved them. He had never been so praised in his life, the fool," she scoffed. "And he couldn't bear to lose it."

"He decided it would be easier to just keep Kaveri holding your curse at bay," I said quietly. "Forever?"

The Asura nodded. "He could not find me, and he was too weak and afraid to do the right thing, so he took matters into his own hands. You see, when she had transformed the princess into the urn of water, the witch had been very clear: the urn had to be kept safe. If it were harmed in any way, it would not be possible to transform the princess back. So Jai broke it."

Kaveri's own father had condemned her to an eternity in a lonely prison, holding back a curse for all time while he collected the glory. I never had a father, but I had a grandfather, and I knew there was nothing in any universe that could tempt him to do something like that to *anyone*, let alone his own child.

History lessons and the news had taught me a long time ago that people could be just as awful as any evil mythical creature, but it was still such a difficult thing to swallow. Why was it so much easier when the monsters had horns and antlers?

"The witch was furious," Sura said, pulling my mind back to the empty, dusty lodge. "She punished the king. She clasped his hand and bespelled him, transforming him into a tree on the bank of the river. 'As long as the curse remains unbroken and the princess remains trapped, you will be trapped, too,' she said. And that was the end of the reign of King Jai."

She clasped his hand and bespelled him. Hadn't the gandaberunda shown me the clasped hands of a king and witch? I'd dismissed it as a symbolic part of the story the Good Witch had told us, but I should have guessed it meant something more important.

As for the gandaberunda, I understood now. When it had woken up to help us fight Mahishasura, it had decided to put right one other injustice before going back to sleep. It hadn't been able to undo Natasha's spell and turn Kaveri back into her human self, but it had been able to release her from the riverbed.

Had it known what it was unleashing on the kingdom? A girl made of water, and an old and terrible curse. Had the gandaberunda known how much rage was in Kaveri? Had it known she would lash out? Had it risked that because it had known I would come? Had it been counting on me to fix everything?

But only the gandaberunda could answer those questions for me, and it had already told me everything it wanted to.

"How is she so powerful?" I asked. "Is it just because she's in an elemental form?"

"She was betrayed," said Sura, and I wondered which *she* she was really talking about. "Her fury comes from betrayal, and her power comes from fury. There is terrible power to be found in the dark, worldbuilder, if you have the nerve to seek it. The princess has spent a hundred years looking into the dark. The dark looked back."

I clenched my fists. "So that's it, then? Like you, Kaveri's decided to condemn the kingdom, so there's no way to stop the curse? That's it for this world?"

"Yes," said Sura. "And we will watch it end together."

"That's a very nice invitation, but no," I replied. "I let you bring me here because I wanted to save Kaveri, but now I have to go find a way to save the world. *Again*."

Sura's deer face didn't show emotions the way human faces did, but her eyes did. They were full of amusement as she said, "You must know I cannot allow that, world-builder."

"The others will come for me."

"Not with my beasts standing watch," she replied. "There is not a living creature in the universe that will be able to get past them. As for you," she went on, "I suppose it would be very tedious for me if you kept trying to flee. What shall I do with you?"

I thought for a terrifying moment that she was going to set her beasts on me, but all she did was turn over one of the hands resting on the arms of her chair. There was glitter in her palm, gold and gray, and she blew it at me.

"I told you," she said as I breathed the glitter in and recoiled. "There is power to be found in the dark places of the world. That dust comes from the shadows. It will spell you into obedience. Do not look so afraid," she added. "The effects wear off after a year or two."

A *year* or two? I stared at her in horror. "You can't," I croaked, my throat burning from the dust. *"Please."*

"It is already done." Her voice was almost sympathetic. "Can you not feel it?"

My throat hurt, but otherwise I didn't feel any different. While I looked down at myself as if there might be some transformation on my body, the pale glint of gold caught my eye. Was it the tattoo on my wrist? No, it was the bracelet on top of it, mostly hidden under the sleeve of my coat. The bracelet Jojo had made.

The one that meant no spell or curse would work on me.

"Now," Sura was saying sweetly, "you will be very good and obedient, won't you?"

Every part of me wanted the pleasure and satisfaction of saying, "Actually, no, I won't," and running right out of the lodge, but I had to be smarter than that. If I just ran now, I wouldn't get very far. The beasts were still prowling in and around the lodge. Like she'd said, no living thing would get past them.

I swallowed, pasted an awkward smile on my face, and said, "Of course I'll be obedient."

"There. That's much better." Sura stretched her stiff neck, and her shoulders slumped a little in the chair, like she was exhausted with putting on a show. She gestured to the dusty, empty hearth a few feet away from her chair. "Sit over there and stay put."

This was fine, I told myself as I sat down right beside a cobweb and tried to ignore that the sight of it made my brain itch. This was *good*, in fact. This would give me time to think of a way out.

I didn't know how to find Kaveri, or what I'd do when I did, but I *did* know how to find Natasha. That was the only possible next step. The Not-So-Good Witch was the only one who could give me the answers I needed, if she could only be persuaded to tell me the truth this time.

Well, no, that wasn't my next step. More like my *next* next step. First, I had to get out of here.

I stayed quiet and still for what felt like hours but was probably only minutes. The place where the roof had caved in was open to the sky, and I shivered in the cold, but I was also glad I could see the moon between the trees. It had barely moved since I'd sat down on the hearth (next to the cobweb where a toothy, girl-eating spider was probably lurking, my brain helpfully reminded me), which meant it wasn't as late as it felt.

"Sura," I said meekly, when I couldn't bear to sit still anymore. "I'm not immortal like you. I need to, um, pee."

"What is pee?"

"I need to use the bathroom," I explained. "And eat."

She twitched her head ever so slightly to the left and looked at me out of the corner of her eye. It was like even the smallest movements were difficult for her. Startled, I realized I felt sorry for her.

"It has been some time since I last dined with humans," the Asura said doubtfully. "What do you eat?"

"Berries will work," I said, thinking quickly. "If I go outside, I could look for berries there."

"Then do that," she said. "Return as soon as you are finished."

"Of course."

I was halfway to the door when she added, "Two of my beasts will go with you."

Not *great* news, but I'd expected the beasts to be around no matter where I went. The important thing was getting into the forest without rousing Sura's suspicions.

I couldn't risk mounting the clockwork horse, and I didn't stand a chance on foot against an entire army of beasts hunting me down, but if I was lucky, I might be able to get away from just *two* of them.

I trod cautiously down the rotten wooden stairs outside the lodge and, with two glowing fox-beasts at my heels, started for the nearest trees.

My brain prodded at me, hurtling miles ahead as always. Even if I got away from Sura and the creatures, how would I find my way out of the Magicwood? Were the Crows trying to find me right now? Would we miss each other? What if they tried to rescue me and Sura's beasts got them? Would I wander the woods alone until my sad and untimely demise? Would Mum be so furious that she would resurrect my ghost just so she could murder me herself?

I batted the anxious, clawing questions away. *One thing at a time, for heaven's sake.*

The real problem to solve was how I was going to get away from the two fox-beasts. I couldn't outrun them, but could I distract them? How? Would they even leave me alone long enough for me to set up some kind of distraction?

I was halfway between the stilts holding up the lodge and the trees of the forest when I saw a movement out of the corner of my eye. Unlike the graceful, glowing beasts prowling and pacing around the stairs and stilts, this movement was shadowy and jerky. I turned my head curiously and spotted a blurry, terrified face looking out at me from behind the closest stilt.

I almost tripped over my own feet.

Stumbling, I used the opportunity to tug loose the laces of one shoe. I backtracked a few steps and, feeling quite sure that Sura had no idea how laces worked, pretended that the only way I could retie my shoe was by leaning on the stilt for support.

"Joy?" I whispered.

The ghost stuck his head round the stilt. From the little I could see of his face, he looked more scared than glum for once. "I c-came to t-tell you that y-you need to go that w-way." He jerked his head in the opposite direction I'd been walking in before. "Once you're in the shelter of the t-trees, run."

His teeth were chattering with fear rather than because of the cold. My heart gave a sympathetic thump. Yes, he was a ghost who didn't have to worry about getting killed, and yes, he'd run away from trouble in spite of that, but didn't I know what it was like to be afraid?

"I can't just run," I mumbled, keeping my chin tucked against my chest as I sloooowly retied my laces. "They'll come after me. I can't outrun them."

"You have t-to," he said. "They t-told me to t-tell you that."

"But—"

"I c-can't stay. I n-need to g-go."

I watched him simply vanish into thin air. How had he even gotten past the beasts? How had he gone so completely unnoticed that he'd not only gotten past them but had stayed hidden in spite of the glowing beasts weaving around the stilts? Hadn't Sura told me no living thing would—

Oh. Of course. No *living* thing. Was it possible that Sura and the beasts couldn't see Joy?

I thought of how Pip had swooped down at the beasts in the forest earlier tonight, over and over, his beak and talons outstretched, and how each time the beasts never seemed to expect him before he struck. They couldn't see *him*, either.

Dropping my foot back to the ground, I stepped out

from under the lodge and started walking in the direction Joy had told me to go. I risked a nervous glance up into the sky, and there he was, a crow flying overhead.

Okay, maybe it was just a regular crow, but I was sure it was Pip. He probably hadn't figured out that the beasts couldn't see him or else he'd have come closer, but he was here. He and the others had sent Joy past the beasts to tell me where to go.

But I still couldn't outrun the foxes at my heels, or the rest of the beasts who would take up the chase as soon as the foxes saw me bolt. Maybe the Crows had a plan, but I knew that whatever it was, they couldn't possibly be close enough to help me outpace unearthly, immortal beasts. If they were, the beasts would have sensed their presence.

So I went back to my distraction idea. What if, in the mere seconds of cover I'd have when I stepped into the trees, I could somehow throw the beasts off my trail?

I still had my pencils, so maybe I could draw something? No, I wouldn't have enough time for that.

But I didn't have anything else—

Wait. What about my phone?

Five steps to the cover of the trees. Four steps. Three.

Was that my heart pounding so loudly I was sure

even Sura would be able to hear it from all the way up in her hall?

I pulled my phone out of my pocket. I almost dropped it, my hand unsteady and my thumb swiping blindly across the screen, but I managed to get it unlocked and cued up a video Mum had taken of me on my birthday.

Two steps. One.

Now.

As soon as I stepped into the shadows of the trees, I ducked into the overgrowth, tapped the play icon on the video, and threw my phone with all my strength. As it sailed through the air and vanished into the darkness, I heard the sound of my own tinny voice fading with it.

There was a second of startled silence, and then came the shrill keen of the beasts, the sound of Sura's furious scream. They followed the sound of my voice, just as I'd hoped, and the moment they were out of sight, I started to run. They'd hear me and turn back, but I'd bought myself a few precious seconds.

The spaces between the trees widened, and I ran faster, each breath short and painful, my feet slamming into the dry, knotted overgrowth. Moments later, the sound of light, fast paws echoed close behind me, and I could *feel* the chill of their frosty, crystalline breath, but I was still ahead—

Then something streaked down from above. I'd just caught a glimpse of its winged shadow on the forest floor in front of me before something grabbed me under the arms and hoisted me into the air.

I screamed.

"Ouch!" said an annoyed voice.

"Lej?!"

"Who else?"

"The last time this happened to me, it was a winged Asura snatching me up for Mahishasura, so I'm sorry for experiencing a *teeny* smidge of panic!"

I couldn't see him rolling his eyes, but I knew he was. I kept *my* eyes squeezed firmly shut. I knew that if I looked down and saw just how high off the ground we probably were, I'd panic and flail and that would be the end of us. With my eyes closed, I could convince myself that I was totally and completely fine. And even though I knew I wasn't, relief flooded through me anyway. Sura and her beasts couldn't reach me up here.

Something creaked and shuddered. My eyes flew open

in time to see the mountains dropping away from us, but now the height was the least of my concerns. "Was that—"

"The wings can't hold us both up," Lej said shortly. "It's okay. We just need to make it back to the others. It's not far as the crow flies. No pun intended."

Resisting the temptation to scream some more, I gripped his arm tightly with both hands.

I could practically *hear* him wince. "Is that making you feel better?"

"No," I informed him. "I'm holding on just in case you decide to let me go and save yourself. I'm warning you, it won't be easy to shake me off."

The shuddering of the wings grew more violent. I closed my eyes, bracing myself for the worst, only to realize an instant later that the movement was just Lej's laughter.

"You're the most ridiculous human I've ever met, Kiki Kallira," he said. "But I'm glad you're around."

19

We got lucky. The wings gave out just as we approached the clearing where the chariot had crashed. The shuddering of the mechanics in the wings turned into rattling, wheezing sounds, and then, with a final creak, the wings flopped over Lej's shoulders. We both yelled as we tumbled the rest of the way to the ground.

Then there were more yells, of alarm *and* delight. Groaning, feeling like literally every single part of me was bruised, I rolled over and let Suki help me up.

Pip landed on my shoulders. "Told you we could do it," he said to the others, fluffing his feathers and preening. "Just so you know, Kiki, it was my idea."

"I'm shocked," I said, lifting him down into my arms

and hugging him. "*Shocked.* You're telling me *you* came up with such a madcap rescue? You, the king of fun and tomfoolery?"

"Have I been promoted from captain to king?" Pip sounded gleeful. "Have I peaked? Is there anything better than a king?"

"A queen," came Chamundeshwari's dry voice.

I turned and immediately had my face licked by a lion. Sputtering, I let go of Pip and put my arms around Simha instead. He and Chamundeshwari were both safe and had obviously tracked us down at some point after I'd left. Jojo, too, seemed to be in much better shape than before. He was back in his chair and had a sizeable bump on his head, but he was smiling at me.

"I'm *so* glad you're back!" Suki said fiercely. "You gave me such a fright! I was so sure you'd sacrificed yourself for us, and I was totally spitting *furious* with you—"

My smile fell away as the memory of the past few hours came rushing back. "I've got a lot to tell you."

"Tell us while we get out of here," Lej said. "You can fix the chariot, can't you? We gained a fair bit of distance on the beasts by flying, but they'll catch up sooner or later."

I was achy and shaken and wanted to sleep for a hundred years, but I got my pencils out of my pocket and got to work. The sooner we got out of the Magicwood, the better.

As I drew new seams between the broken pieces of our chariot, patched it back up, and sketched new horses out of the dry, cracked earth beneath our feet (well, creatures more or less shaped like horses, anyway), I told the others everything about Sura and Kaveri.

There was silence when I finished. Even Joy, who was back, seemed to be at a loss. Pip was the one who spoke first.

"So you're telling me we have a missing princess who can drown people, a ghost with unfinished business, *and* an Asura with a broken heart on our hands?" he demanded. "What's next, a golden goose? A stolen firstborn child?"

"Wait, what?" Suki interjected, looking worried. "I was born three minutes before my sister. I don't want to be stolen!"

"There will be no golden geese," I said firmly, though it wasn't like I could actually promise that. For all I knew, there could be a golden, silver, or just a plain feathered goose waiting for us back at Crow House! "And no stolen first-born children, either. Pip just means that this feels like a fairy tale."

"Right down to the wicked witch," said Pip bitterly.

I didn't reply. Natasha hadn't betrayed us the way Ashwini had, and I hadn't loved or trusted her the way I had loved and trusted Ashwini, either, but the confusion, anger, and hurt I felt right then was a little too familiar. Natasha had lied to us. She'd let us confront Sura and an army of ferocious beasts just so we could rescue someone she'd *known* we wouldn't find. And I couldn't understand why.

But I would find out. One way or another, I'd make her explain.

We righted the newly repaired chariot and hitched the cracked, earthy horses to it. They were *really* creepy.

Chamundeshwari took the reins. "Rest," she told us. "Simha and I will see us safely home."

But I couldn't rest, and I didn't think I was the only one. My mind wouldn't switch itself off. I wondered if Samara was okay. I wondered if the gandaberunda had made a terrible mistake when it had trusted me to fix everything. I wondered how I was supposed to fix *anything* if no one told me the truth.

How could the curse be broken? The easiest way, of course, was by Sura revoking it, but she would never do that. She couldn't be killed, so the curse couldn't be revoked that way, either. As for Kaveri, I still only had pieces of her story, but one thing I *did* know was that she'd tried to drown me, so I doubted we'd get any help from her. I wasn't even sure we could stop her. How do you stop someone who can turn herself into tempests and storms?

The only other option I could think of was getting Natasha to transform someone *else* into an urn of water, but that just felt like history repeating itself. Natasha would probably refuse to do it, and in any case, who exactly was supposed to make that sacrifice after everything we'd just discovered?

I was out of ideas, but there was still that *next* next step: confronting Natasha. She was the only one who could help us now.

It was just after dawn when, tired and dejected, we arrived at last outside Crow House. Simha, who seemed to have no limits to his energy, announced that he was going to put the kettle on for tea and bounded into the house.

The rest of us trudged into the front room—

And froze.

There was someone in Crow House already. A glaring, furious someone.

"Well, this is a pickle," said Pip.

I let out a squeak of horror. *"Mum?"*

20

Nope. Nuh-uh. Absolutely not. This does not compute.

My brain was having none of it.

"How—" I spluttered. "When—what—*how*—"

My mother was sitting on the sofa. She didn't speak; she just *glared*.

"You told me Emily couldn't come with us because this universe was keyed to me!" I said to Lej, feeling tremendously betrayed.

"She's your *mother*," Lej said defensively, looking every bit as surprised as I was. "The boundaries obviously recognized her as part of you. Or you as part of her."

"But time was supposed to stay frozen while I was here!"

"I don't know what to tell you, Kiki. I don't get it, either."

Mum *still* hadn't said a word. The other Crows, crowded in the doorway with us, watched us in wide-eyed silence.

"It was Lej's fault!" I blurted out.

Pip choked on a laugh and hastily covered it up with an extremely fake-sounding sneeze.

Lej scowled at me. "Are you kidding me?"

I shrugged sheepishly. "I panicked! Mum's giving me the Look. I'm a total wimp when she gives me the Look!"

It was true. My spine crumbled like a cookie in the face of my mother's wrath. She almost never got *really* angry with me, but when she did, it was terrifying. How did she do it? Had she taken special lessons at Mum School?

I made a brave attempt to reassemble my spine. "Mum, the thing is, I, um—"

Mum's eyes narrowed just a fraction, and I almost lost my nerve. Her eyebrows lifted. "Yes, my precious bean?" she said very sweetly. "What is the thing?"

"Well, um, the Kikiverse is in trouble. I had to come help."

"I see," she said in the voice of someone who very much did not see. "And you, my only child, the cherub of my heart, decided not to share this important decision with me?"

How was the sugary, quiet voice so much scarier than yelling? It made no sense!

"You weren't supposed to know I was gone!" I burst out. "It was supposed to be like last time, when I got home and no time at all had passed in the other universe!"

"Well, time *did* pass, Kiki!" Mum exploded, standing up. "I came to your room to say goodnight, and you weren't there! Worse, I literally *saw* you vanish into that sketchbook! I had no idea what would become of you! What did you expect me to do, just sit around twiddling my thumbs until you came back? *If* you came back at all?"

The fear and pain in her voice were deep, and I felt absolutely *awful* because I knew how afraid she was of losing someone else she loved.

"I'm so sorry. I should have told you." I took a step closer to her. "Didn't Emily explain?"

"She tried," said Mum.

"But what did you do?" I asked.

"*Do*? I followed you!"

"No, before that," I said, confused. "It took you three days to come after me, so you must've tried something else first."

"Three days?" Now Mum was the one who looked confused. "You only left last night."

"No, I didn't," I said. "Lej, Pip, and I left on Tuesday night. It's Friday morning."

"It's *Wednesday* morning," Mum said. "Emily and I sat up all night trying to figure out what to do, waiting for you to return, but when morning came and there was still no sign of you, I'd had enough. Emily told me how you'd entered the sketchbook, so I tried it and it worked. Once I got here, some *very* nice people pointed me this way," she added. "They don't seem especially happy with you at the moment, but as your mother, it seems I'm something of a celebrity in this universe."

I turned to look at the Crows, all of whom looked as bewildered as I was. "We *have* been here three nights," I said slowly, "but only *one* night passed in the other world."

"Time didn't stop like you expected it to," Pip said.

"But it *did* slow down."

Jojo suddenly went rigid in his chair. "It's you," he said

to me. "It must be. The way time works is based on your connection to this universe."

"The longer this universe exists on its own, the less powerful my connection to it is," I finished the thought for him, my heart sinking at a new reminder that the Kiki-verse was becoming less and less *mine* with each day. "But I still *have* a connection to it, so the time thing is all messy now. That's why only a day passed there while three days passed here."

"I'm so confused," said Mum. "Scientifically, none of this makes sense."

"That part is Kiki's fault," Lej said helpfully. "I don't think science is her thing."

"Kiki, come here," Jojo said, ignoring everyone.

I obeyed, but immediately regretted it when Jojo yanked a few hairs out of my head. "Ow!"

"Got to go," he said excitedly, wheeling himself out of the room.

He'd been gone a scant second when Simha pushed his way in. "The tea is getting cold. What are you all doing in—oh, my word! A grown-up!"

Poor Mum's eyes almost popped out of her head. "You weren't kidding about the lion, then," she said faintly.

"I am the mighty Simha," said Simha proudly. "May I offer you tea?"

He trotted out of the room without waiting for an answer, possibly assuming that no one in their right mind would refuse tea, and Mum blinked at the doorway like she was quite certain she would wake up any minute and all this would be over.

There was a pause, and then Mum, recovering from this latest shock, noticed how ragged and filthy we were. "Why do you all look like you've been involved in something dangerous? And why do *you* look so happy?"

This last remark was said to Suki, who was beaming from ear to ear. "It's just so *nice* to have a mother around!"

That was it. Mum gasped, her face crumpled, and the next thing I knew, she had her arms around Suki *and* Lej, a turn of events that Suki was obviously thrilled with, if the enthusiasm with which she returned the hug was any indication. Lej put up a very half-hearted struggle.

"You poor, sweet babies," Mum said tenderly, obviously overcome by the tragic plight of the motherless orphans. Meanwhile, the motherless orphans were milking the situation for all it was worth. "What you need is a big delicious breakfast."

"We do need that," said Suki with no shame at all, nodding vigorously. "We are very sweet, hungry babies."

"Then get cleaned up while I cook," Mum suggested.

"*Can* we get cleaned up?" I asked the others anxiously, my skin crawling at the mere thought of not being able to get all the dust, sweat, and dirt off me. "Is it safe to?"

"We have some water stockpiled in the tank," said Lej. "As long as we use the timer on the shower door, we should be okay."

There was an unspoken *for now* at the end of his sentence, which was a grim reminder that we were almost out of time.

By the time I stumbled, half asleep, out of a very hasty shower, Mum had joined forces with Simha in the kitchen. I expected them to be chopping, cooking, and complaining about the trials and tribulations of having wayward children, but they'd obviously covered that part already. In fact, it sounded more like—

"Mum!" I froze in the doorway, aghast. "Are you *tickling* Simha?"

"You're the most beautiful thing I've ever seen," Mum was saying. "Your fur is *so* soft, and you have such a *lovely* mane!"

"Simha is a lion!" I objected. "A *warrior* lion!"

"Tell me more about my mane," Simha interrupted me, preening. "It simply isn't appreciated enough. And you can keep rubbing my belly just so," he added hastily when Mum looked like she might stop.

"Now you've done it," said Lej, watching this display over a plate of bacon, sausages, and fried tomatoes. "He'll be intolerable after this."

I was far more exhausted than I was hungry, so I went back to the living room, curled up on the sofa, and closed my eyes for just *one* minute—

—only to wake up with a much brighter sun streaming in through the window and Mum's hand on my shoulder.

"It's just me," she said as I startled. "I didn't want to wake you, but I think we need to talk."

"Did the others tell you anything?" I asked, my voice groggy. My head was slowly filling up with all the things I'd been allowed to forget about while I'd slept.

Mum sighed. "I think they've told me most of it. You *do* know you're coming home with me, don't you?"

"I can't," I said. "I'm sorry I scared you, and I should have told you the truth, but I *can't* go home with you yet. I have to fix this."

"Oh, Kiki," she said, sounding frustrated. "Why do *you* have to be the one to break this curse?"

"Are you saying I should just abandon the Crows?" I asked, sitting upright.

"If you have to, yes! I'm not going to pretend I'm being anything other than selfish, Kiki. *You're* the one I have to protect. I need you to come home, where you're safe."

My throat closed up. "Home isn't any safer, Mum. Dad was home when we lost *him*."

Her face whitened and her lips pressed together, but she said very calmly, "This isn't about him. This is about you thinking you can save everybody just because you did it once. It's about you thinking you have to do this because you think it's the only way to prove that you're strong and brave and all the things *I* already know you are."

"*I* know I'm those things, too," I said, and it was the truth. Yes, I doubted myself a lot. Yes, I was always afraid I'd fail. But I also knew, deep down, that I *was* brave and I *was* strong. I'd discovered that when I'd faced Mahishasura, and I'd proven it every day since. "That's not why I have to finish this. They need me."

Mum's voice was very gentle as she said, "I see."

I didn't like the way she'd said that. "What?"

"You're afraid they *don't* need you."

That hit me somewhere so deep and true that I stood up abruptly. There was a fierce, scratchy *something* in my brain, and I had to stop it in its tracks before it got its claws right into me.

For the first time in my entire life, I couldn't bear to be in the same room as Mum.

"Staying is the right thing to do," I said. I wanted my voice to be cold and calm, but it wobbled. "I'm going to go talk to the Good Witch."

"Kiki, don't—"

I fled before she could say anything else.

21

Eyes straight ahead, Kiki. The Good Witch had lied to us. I needed to find out why. It was time to confront her.

Also, I needed to yell at *somebody*.

"So," said a merry voice above my left ear, accompanied by the brush of a wing. "You're sneaking out of Crow House. I'm following you. Just like old times!"

"Go away, Pip."

"How about no?"

"Pip!"

"Oooh, shouty voice. I guess I'd better think about it, then. Hmm. What a pickle. Whatever shall I do?"

In spite of myself, a small smile tugged at the corners

of my mouth, and I glanced up at him, flying right above me. "You're a pest."

We took the bus to the now-familiar Artists' Quarter, and from there to the stop outside the Witches' Guild. This time, we walked *around* Lake Lune. The water looked quiet today, but it wasn't worth the risk of getting in another boat. (The boat! I still had the piece of wood back at Crow House. So much had happened that I'd almost forgotten I still needed to re-create the fisherman's lost boat.)

In the room at the top of the lighthouse, we found Natasha waiting for us, like she'd known we would come sooner or later.

After hours of picturing exactly what I would say to her, after hours of whole conversations conducted in my mind, after hours of planning just how I would shout and yell, only one word burst violently out of me.

"Why?"

"I was sixteen years old," she said. "I did not know any better."

"I don't think you did anything wrong *then*," I said furiously. "You didn't know what King Jai was going to do! But now? Now's a bit different, isn't it? You knew Kaveri wasn't Sura's prisoner. Why did you send us into the Magicwood? Why didn't you just tell us the truth?"

Her Epic Majesty, our beloved Saint Natasha, is not always right about everything. That was what Anya, the young witch, had said when we'd stumbled across her storming out of the Witches' Guild. She'd been angry that the guild kept acting like Natasha could do no wrong. Maybe I should have paid attention. Maybe I should have seen this coming.

There was no guilt or shame on Natasha's face as she said simply, "If I had told you everything, you would have gone looking for Kaveri instead of looking for Sura."

"You think?" Pip retorted. "The brave, sweet princess you conjured up for us doesn't exist. She almost drowned Kiki and Lej right out there in the lake! Just because! No one in this kingdom is safe with her out there. Compared to her, Sura is toothless."

"Sura could remove her curse at any time but chooses not to," Natasha said coldly. "That does not seem toothless to me. Kaveri, on the other hand, is a monster of *my* making."

I couldn't accept that. "But the lives of everyone in the kingdom—"

"I'd hoped you would save them," she said. "I sent you to Sura because I hoped you might find a way to defeat her and break the curse. It is not my fault that you failed."

Pip, who pretty much never lost his temper, almost exploded. "You do *not* get to blame us for this!"

You will fail. You failed. Those words were always at my heels, and it looked like I just couldn't outrun them.

But I was also angry, and for once, it wasn't with myself. "I'd be a lot less likely to fail if people would just tell me the truth," I snapped. "Or better yet, *ask* me first. The gandaberunda didn't bother to ask before it set Kaveri loose. You didn't bother to ask before you sent me after Sura. Both of you broke stuff and just hoped I'd fix it for you, but you should have *asked*."

Natasha considered that for a moment, turning the words over in that solemn way she had. "That is true," she said at last, "but after what I did to her, I owe Kaveri a debt. I could not tell you the truth and condemn her any more than I already have."

Something in her voice caught my attention. I stared at her, watching the way her arms were crossed tightly over her chest and the way the glittering light in her purple eyes seemed to have completely vanished. "You were both sixteen," I said slowly. "When she and Jai came to you and asked you to transform her, that wasn't the first time you'd met, was it?"

"No."

"You *knew* her. She was important to you."

"Yes," Natasha said softly. "She was everything I told you she was. I did not lie about that. She was kind and brave. She loved pretty pink things. She was an excellent archer. She loved lying on her back and looking for shapes in the clouds. And she was always so determined to help her people."

I knew what she was trying to do. She wanted us to see Kaveri as the girl she'd once been, not the monster she'd become. But she was *both* of those things, and Natasha couldn't pretend one of them didn't exist.

Pip fluttered down to the desk. "Okay, I'll give you a *little* wiggle room because of what she meant to you, but you know she's not that girl anymore, don't you? Don't you think *that* girl would want you to stop her before she does something she can never take back?"

"And how would I stop her?" asked Natasha. "By trapping her in a riverbed for another hundred years?"

"If we do nothing, the Old Well will go dry, and everyone will—"

"No." There was nothing but steel in Natasha's voice. "I will not help you cage her. I will not do that to her again."

I lost my temper. "Then show me another way to break the curse *and* stop the violent water creature, and I'll do it!"

"Kill Sura."

"Even if I wanted to, I can't!" I snapped. "Her heart was taken from her. She *can't* be killed. So no, we can't break the curse that way, and even if we could, how would that stop Kaveri, who drowns anyone who gets in her way? Why can't you just undo the spell you put on her and transform her back into a girl?"

"Because the spell was bound to the urn, and the urn is lost!" Natasha snapped back. "Jai broke it."

"So there's no other way," said Pip. "You do see that, don't you? I don't *want* to use Kaveri to restore the river, but it does kill two birds with one stone."

"I would have thought you, of all people, wouldn't be so quick to speak of killing birds," Natasha said coldly.

"Okay," I said. "You won't help us. Fine. Will you at least tell us where Kaveri is?"

"Even if I wanted to, I could not. I do not know where she has gone. She is not human, and therefore she is not bound to human rules. She exists as water and, as such, can transform herself into a river, a storm, or a sea. She could be the puddle at your feet, and you would not know it unless she wanted you to. But I do not believe that is what she's doing," Natasha added, her expression distant. "The waters have been too quiet today. I believe she's hidden herself away."

"I guess that's a good thing if it means she's not out there trying to drown someone *else*," said Pip. "On the other hand, we can't restore the river without her, so it would be nice to know where she is."

Natasha said nothing.

"Let's go, Kiki," Pip said quietly. "There's nothing more we can do here."

Feeling lost and defeated, I followed him out of the lighthouse.

In the soft, golden light of the midday sun, it was almost possible to forget that the lake lapping at my feet had been poisoned with salt, or that the Old Well was almost dry, or that my mother was afraid she would lose me, or that—

No, that was a path I could *not* let my mind travel down.

I sat down on the rocks and tossed pebbles into the lake. "I'm all out of next steps, Pip. If Natasha won't help us, we're stuck."

"We'll find a way," Pip said. "We always do. *You* always do."

"Not this time. I think Mum thinks the Kikiverse doesn't need me." I grimaced. "No, that's not quite true. I think *I* think the Kikiverse doesn't need me. I haven't done anything the gandaberunda or the Good Witch or anyone else hoped I would. I keep failing."

"Meh," he said, shrugging his wings. "So what? Everyone fails until they don't."

"Did you read that in a fortune cookie?"

"That bit of wisdom is pure Pip, thanks very much."

He wasn't exactly *wrong*, I suppose. I squinted against the sunlight, trying to construct an answer to an impossible problem. Maybe I needed to throw out everything I knew and start from scratch. Like a piece of art, I had to start with nothing. First, the empty canvas. Then I could pencil in a messy sketch, then a better one, then ink over the lines, then add color, and finally add the shadows and highlights.

Pip landed on my knee. "I don't know if the Kikiverse needs you," he said, his face and beak pointing away from me like he had suddenly found the lake very interesting. "I can't speak for a whole world. Just for myself. And you know how you told me yesterday that I shouldn't stay just for you? Well, the thing is, I'm not. You think I'm still here because you need me, but that's not true. I'm still here because *I* need *you*."

I swallowed. "Really?"

"Cross my heart and hope to—"

"I'm not listening!"

He laughed, but his merry voice was unusually serious as he said, "I don't like thinking of whatever's next. You won't be there."

"But do you hate this? Living as a crow?"

"Well, beaks are awkward, talons tear holes in things, and I can't tinker with stuff the way I used to. It's been *way* too long since I've been able to invent some kind of mischief. But," he went on, "I can fly. And I get to stay. That makes everything else worth it."

I used one fingertip to ruffle the feathers of his head. "Do you think I'm your unfinished business?"

"Well, you're going to be a mess for a good long while, so I hope so."

I pushed him off my knee, but I was laughing. "Stay."

"I will."

"But not always."

"No," he said. "But I'm here now. And I'm not going anywhere yet."

22

A girl with an enormous smile and twin braids threw open the door of the Crow House right before we reached it. I gave her a half-hearted smile in return, but shook my head. "I hope that smile means *you* have some good news, Suki, because we definitely don't."

"Well, actually—"

"Wait," I interrupted. The girl's voice was much quieter than Suki's. I pointed an accusing finger at her. "You're not Suki!"

"No, I'm the other one," Samara said cheerfully, hugging me and kissing Pip on the top of his head. A tiny frown creased her forehead as she stepped back. "You look *awful.*"

"And you don't," I marveled. She looked exactly as I'd last seen her. "Were you really okay inside that book?"

"It was literally the highlight of my whole life."

I smiled. "I bet Suki's cross she spent all that time worrying about you."

"She's a *little* peeved, yes."

"At least one of us had a good time," Pip grumped.

"But if I hadn't gotten myself gobbled up by the Beast Book," said Samara, looking immensely satisfied, "I wouldn't have discovered the thing I've discovered. I'm going to get Jojo to help me bake Numa a cake, by the way. He was very kind when he rescued me from the book."

"Um, we can talk about Numa and cakes later," said Pip incredulously. "What did you discover?"

We followed Samara into the kitchen. There was no sign of Mum or Simha, but the others were clustered around the table. Joy stood slightly apart, looking gloomily out of the kitchen window.

"You're back!" Suki cried. "Yay! Simha had to meet Chamundeshwari at the Summer Palace for a trial, but the rest of us are *planning*. Did you tell them?"

That last bit was addressed to her sister, who replied

with "I was just about to, but I can see you're dying to do it."

"It was *your* discovery," said Suki generously.

"They told me everything when I got back a little while ago," Samara said to Pip and me, her eyes shining. Her talents, like mine, were quieter and less showy than the others', so I knew it always made her incredibly proud to be able to contribute something. "And it made me think of something I saw in the Beast Book. It was you who led me to it, actually, Kiki."

"Me?"

"Do you remember telling Numa something about a Naga king who could control the weather? I was so curious about that that I went looking while I was inside the book, and when I was learning all about him, I also saw all this other stuff about elemental beasts made out of fire, water, and so on."

"There might be a way to trap Kaveri without the Good Witch's help!" Suki burst out, obviously unable to restrain herself for another minute. "We can save the Kikiverse!"

I looked between the twins. "How?"

"We bind Kaveri's power. It's what the people in the

olden days used to do to bind the most violent of the elemental beasts. Once we do that, Kaveri won't be able to transform herself, or hurt or drown anyone, so we'd be able to trap her back in the riverbed."

"And then what?" I asked. Hope battled with unease. "How will this be any different from last time?"

"This time, we *won't* trap her forever," said Lej firmly. "The only way to transform Kaveri back into her human form is to have Natasha undo her original spell, right? Which she can't do without the urn that King Jai broke? But if we had more time and all the resources of the Ancient Library and the Witches' Guild at our disposal, we might discover *another* way to undo the spell. We might be able to free Kaveri for good."

"And we'd also use that extra time to find a way to defeat Sura and break the curse for good," Suki added.

I wanted to be excited, but I was full of doubt. "That's a lot of ifs and maybes."

"It is, but I think it's the only choice we have right now," Jojo said. "The Old Well's almost dry. More than anything, what we need is more time."

I nodded. It wasn't a perfect answer, but they were right. We needed time, and there would be time for better ideas later, when the kingdom was safe. "Did the Beast Book tell you *how* to bind Kaveri?"

"Do you remember telling us there was a gold ring around the neck of the urn in the vision the gandaberunda showed you?" asked Samara. "It's called a binding ring. Natasha needed it for her original spell, and we need it for ours. Lej can find the parts we need, and Suki should be able to do the alchemy. Between them, and maybe with some help from the Witches' Guild, I think they can create the ring. If they can, and then if we can somehow get the ring around Kaveri's wrist, she'll be bound."

"Oh, is *that* all?" Pip said. He flopped over on the table, throwing a dramatic wing over his face. "Is no one else concerned about the part where we'll have to get *close* to a monstrous water princess to pull this off? No one?"

"Maybe you or Joy could do it," said Lej drily. "You know, what with both of you being dead and having a lot less to lose."

"I must regretfully decline," said Joy at once. "In fact, I would go so far as to insist that I absolutely should not go anywhere *near* her."

We ignored that. I focused on the plan. "Okay, Lej and

the twins might as well get to work on the gold ring. Once Simha gets back from the trial, he might be able to help us find Kaveri. He and Chamundeshwari have powers we don't have."

"And while you're all doing that," Jojo added, "I need everyone's bracelets. The ones I gave you before we went into the Magicwood. There's something I need to add to them before we go up against any more monsters."

He wheeled himself off to his room as soon as we'd handed over the bracelets. Lej and the twins headed out to see if the Witches' Guild would help us forge the binding ring, while Pip fluttered around the kitchen in search of a snack. I wasn't sure when Simha would be back, so I decided to go find Mum. I couldn't avoid her forever.

I wasn't sure how, but I ended up in Pip's old room instead. Crow House had kept it exactly as he'd left it, so it looked like Pip still lived there. It was the room of both our childhoods, filled with all the relics of the adventures we'd gone on when we'd been younger. Adventures I'd made up and adventures he'd dreamed about. Long before we'd known the other one was real, we'd known each other.

There was an overflowing treasure chest from that time we were pirates and a sword we'd used when we'd been princesses slaying dragons. A tree grew right into the wall, with our treehouse perched in the branches, and a book filled with our childish scribbles sat on a table beside what looked suspiciously like a half-finished stink bomb. I bent down to pick up Petey, a duplicate of the much-loved stuffed rabbit I'd lost in my universe a few years ago. He was coming home with me this time.

Mum found me a moment later. I watched her eyes travel around the room, widening in recognition. "He really *is* your Pip," she said in wonder. "I remember picking you up after school, back when you were little, and you'd tell me these stories about all the adventures you and he went on."

"Remember this?" I held Petey up.

"Petey," she said, smiling. "You were inconsolable when you lost him."

I gave her a tentative smile. "You know, this world is kind of yours, too. It wouldn't be what it is if it weren't for you."

"Then I'm incredibly proud of myself," she said, ruffling my hair. "And you, of course, but I hope you knew that already."

"Sorry I stormed out before."

She laughed. "You're twelve. It was bound to happen sooner or later."

"Um, and I should probably mention I lost my phone. Actually, I threw it."

"We'll come back to *that* later," Mum said. There were golden lion hairs on her leggings and oversized sweatshirt, and she picked a few of them off before sitting down on the window seat. Her eyes searched mine. "Do you want to talk about why you stormed out?"

"It was what you said about being afraid that they don't need me anymore," I admitted. "This world, the whole Kikiverse, it's becoming less *me* and more something else. Itself, I guess."

"You created it," she said. "It lived inside you, and then it took on a life of its own, and now it's not yours anymore. It's a difficult thing to come to terms with."

"You say that like you know what it's like to—*oh*." I gave her a sheepish look. "You mean me."

She smiled. "Like I said, it was bound to happen sooner

or later. And the point is, I do understand how you feel. I know you're afraid you're losing this world, but I don't think you ever could."

"It's just that I *matter* here," I told her, and my face grew hot because it wasn't an easy thing to admit. "When Lej came to London to ask me for my help, it felt nice because it meant I'm someone they can count on. I'm someone who can *do* things, important things. I have actual *magic* here. I mean, how amazing is that?"

"It's ridiculously amazing," she agreed.

"And, well, this is where I discovered that I'm smart and strong and brave and all the things I thought I wasn't. This is where I finally understood that there's nothing wrong with me just because my brain works a bit differently." I picked at the frayed end of my thumbnail and then made myself say the last bit. "I *like* that I'm powerful here. But the more the Kikiverse grows away from me, the less powerful I get."

Mum let out a slow breath. She was quiet for a moment, like she was trying to find the right way to say something. "Kiki, you and I are women with brown skin," she said at last. "I'm sure you've figured out by now that in our universe, people like us don't often get to feel powerful."

"I know."

"And I wish that weren't true, but it is. At least for now. We have to fight for our place in the world. *But,*" she went on firmly, "no matter what universe you're in and no matter how much or how little power you have, some things will always stay the same. Your kindness. Your strength. Your creativity."

"My obsessions and anxiousness," I said ruefully.

"That, too," she said. "You are who you are because of *all* of you, my darling. Trust that it'll see you through anything that comes your way. In *any* world."

I sat down in the window seat beside her. "You know, I think maybe that's just what I needed to hear."

"I *am* your mother. I've gotten pretty good at it."

"The best."

She looked out of the window and absently picked a twig out of my hair. "Your castle in the sky surprised me when I first saw it," she said, smiling wistfully up at it. "It looks so much like Craigievar Castle in Scotland. That's where your dad took me on our first date. You've got a picture of us outside the castle up on your bedroom wall."

"I do," I said, almost surprised. "I mean, I know I do,

but I've had it on my wall for so long that I guess I don't notice it anymore, you know? It's pink and pastel like a fairy-tale castle, isn't it? I must have been thinking about it when I dreamed up the one in the sky."

"We should go back there so you can see it for yourself. You were obsessed with it when you were little." I had absolutely no memory of this, but it was delightful to hear about. "You called yourself the Dragon-Slaying Princess of Craigievar and *demanded* I draw pictures of you in your castle."

I started laughing, but then the words she just said replayed themselves in my head, and my laughter broke off abruptly.

"Oh. *Oh*."

"Kiki?" Mum frowned at me. "Are you okay?"

I jumped off the window seat and practically bounced up and down, pointing frantically at the window. "I know where she is! I know where she is!"

"Who? Kaveri?" Mum stared. "Where?"

I kept pointing. "Where would a princess go if she wanted to hide from the world?"

Mum turned to look back up into the sky. "You think she's up there? In your castle?"

"A princess who loved pink pretty things? A princess who loved looking for shapes in the clouds? I *know* she's up there!"

"And I suppose you're going to go after her," she said, worry creating little furrows between her eyebrows. "No, sorry, let me rephrase that. I suppose *we* are going to go after her."

"You're going to come with me?" I asked, startled.

She raised her eyebrows. "Have you given me much of a choice? You won't come home with me until you've saved the world, and I can't and won't force you to, so that leaves me in a bit of a bind, doesn't it? Do you think I should sit here and sip Simha's excellent tea while my only child goes to confront a violent princess who may or may not try to drown her for a second time?"

"Well, I guess when you put it like *that*—"

"I have one question, however," said Mum. "How exactly are we going to *get* to your castle in the sky?"

I grinned. "I have a chariot," I told her. "And more importantly, I have a pencil. Want to watch me draw some wings to life?"

23

"I do not like this," Joy informed us. "I do not like it one bit. In fact, I would go so far as to say I hate it."

Her face buried in her hands, Samara said in a muffled voice, "I kind of hate it, too."

"THIS. IS. AMAZING!" Suki shrieked at the top of her lungs, and Pip, circling around us, laughed at her and cawed even louder.

We were in the chariot. In the *air*.

Lej and the twins had gotten back from the Witches' Guild late in the afternoon, triumphantly brandishing a newly crafted gold binding ring. Pip, Jojo, and I had just as triumphantly brandished my revelation that Kaveri was in the castle in the clouds.

Unsurprisingly, Lej hadn't felt quite as certain of this as I was, but even he had admitted that it couldn't hurt to check. We'd thought about waiting for Simha and Chamundeshwari to finish with the trial so that they could come with us, but when hours had passed with no sign of them and a friend of Suki's stopped by with the news that a grumbling crowd had gathered outside Sentinel's Tower, we'd decided to just go ahead. Time, after all, was the one thing we didn't have.

So once Jojo had returned our bracelets to us and had provided Mum with one of her very own, he and the other Crows had armed themselves, Pip had been given the binding ring to keep safe because he had the best chance of putting it on Kaveri's wrist, and I had drawn large feathered wings on the chariot *and* on each of the horses. ("If they have wings, are they still horses?" Mum had asked me. "Aren't they now technically pegasi?")

Now we were in the air, and the chariot kept jolting and dropping because the wings were struggling. There had been no time to consult Dev and Archie at the workshop about the proper physics and engineering of wings, so I'd had to just make it up as I'd gone along, and now I wasn't entirely sure they'd hold us up the whole way.

Which was why Joy was hiding under one of the chariot benches, Samara had her hands over her face, and Suki was somehow having the time of her life. Mum, Jojo, and Lej, I noticed, were all gripping the sides of the chariot a little *too* tightly. It was obvious none of them had any faith in my skills as an architect of flying horses and chariots, which was fair because I didn't, either.

But I found that it was weirdly difficult to worry about the wings, because I was too busy worrying about what was waiting for us in the castle above. As the horses flew higher and higher, my whole body tightened with dread. I knew what Kaveri was capable of. I knew what she could do to us if she chose to.

You're out of time, my brain said. *If you fail again, the Kikiverse won't be around to give you another chance.*

Thanks, brain. No pressure or anything.

"Kiki," Suki said quietly, her voice suddenly anything but excited. "I think you were right about where Kaveri is."

I looked up, past Suki's wide eyes and Mum's deathly pale face, past the horses, and gulped.

Where a second ago there had only been a clear golden sky between us and the pink castle, there was now something else. Something cold, dark, and entirely unnatural, a ferocious storm contained in one place—and it was coming right for us.

A bolt of lightning lashed out of the storm, striking down at us. Suki shrieked, and everyone dove for cover. Without thinking, I made a slash with my pencil across the air in front of me, and a second lightning bolt leaped from the tip, deflecting the first.

Quickly, I sketched a shield above us, something to protect us from the lightning, but there was nothing I could do about the storm itself. It was Kaveri's rage, and it was coming, relentless and inevitable, just like the tempest on Lake Lune.

I choked on my terror, scrambling for something, *anything*, that might save us, but I was out of ideas.

The storm loomed, tossing Pip out of the way and snatching one of the horses into the maelstrom. I watched in both awe and horror as the horse crumbled back into earth and twigs and feathers.

Meanwhile, the second horse wobbled off-balance and the chariot lurched, almost tipping Mum right out of it, but Lej grabbed hold of her arm and the horse pushed valiantly on. The storm was seconds away from engulfing us.

Then, out of nowhere, there was a flare of golden light, so blindingly bright that I had to shield my eyes.

The chariot was unsteady, but it had stopped lurching. The single horse kept flying.

I uncovered my eyes.

The storm was gone.

And the Good Witch was standing at the back of the chariot, her outstretched palms glowing with golden light.

Breathless and stunned, I goggled at her for a full minute. "You're here! You came!"

Natasha pressed her lips into a line. "It's like the bird said," she said, nodding her head at Pip, who looked none the worse for having been tossed about in a storm. "Kaveri once loved this kingdom more than anything. What would *that* girl want me to do?"

"You're doing the right thing," Jojo said kindly.

Beside him, Samara had crouched down to try to coax a trembling Joy out of hiding. Natasha eyed the back of his burrowed head with disfavor. "What is that?"

"A ghost," I said. "He's scared, which is kind of understandable. Don't be mean to him."

"You must be Kiki's mother," Natasha went on, turning to Mum. I was somewhat unnerved by how alike they looked side by side.

Mum looked shaken and shocked, but she remembered her manners. "Hello. I'm Natasha."

"Impossible," the Good Witch said at once, affronted. "*I* am Natasha."

"More than one person can be called that, you know," Pip pointed out.

"No, I will not allow it."

Mum looked like she couldn't decide whether to be alarmed or amused. "If it helps, I almost never go by my full name," she told the Good Witch. "My friends call me Nat, and my family calls me Tasha. You're welcome to use either of those."

"Gnat," said the Good Witch, spreading out her skirts and settling down on the back bench with the imperiousness of a queen. "Like the insect? That, I am content with. You can be Gnat."

The chariot groaned and rattled, tilting sideways as the one remaining horse gave up, its wings drooping limply at its sides. Seconds later, it crumbled like the first horse had, bits of dirt and earth fluttering away in the wind.

"Oh, *that's* not good," Pip remarked.

I sent a pleading look at Natasha behind me. She let out a very put-upon sigh, but she waved a hand and guided the chariot safely through the open doors of a balcony off one of the castle turrets.

The chariot clattered onto the pale wooden floor of an enormous empty room, where the walls were made out of the same pink stone as the castle and the doors were the same polished wood of the floor. There was absolutely nothing in the room, not even a cobweb, and this made the dreamy pink of the walls and polished wood of the floors feel somehow hollow and lonely.

It was quiet, too. Wherever Kaveri was, we couldn't hear her, and I was pretty sure that wasn't a good thing. Natasha had told us she could be a puddle at our feet and we'd never know it. She could *easily* sneak up on us.

"There's nothing out there, either," Pip said. He had already flown through the doors on both sides of the room by the time the rest of us got out of the chariot. The room was so empty, his voice echoed. "Not even dust. Didn't you ever come up with ideas for the inside, Kiki?"

"I don't think I did," I said. "And the magic only filled

in the necessary gaps, so it must not have bothered with this."

It made me feel a little sad that the fairy-tale castle of my childhood was empty. And it made me feel sad, too, that Kaveri had come here. A lonely girl in a lonely place.

I squashed the unease and uncertainty I could feel tugging at the back of my mind.

"Joy," Samara was saying gently behind me. I turned. "We're in the castle. You can come out now."

Reluctantly, the ghost edged out from under the chariot bench and stood up. He kept his head down, avoiding everyone's eyes. I thought that it was because he felt ashamed for hiding the whole way up here, but then I saw the expression on the Good Witch's face.

She had gone bone white, her purple eyes sparking with fury. "*You*," she hissed.

Joy said nothing, his shoulders hunched.

"You know Joy?" Lej asked Natasha suspiciously.

Her lips pressed tightly together. Without taking her eyes off the ghost, she addressed the rest of us in a voice that trembled with uncontrollable anger. "What have you done? Where did you find him? *Why* did you bring him here?"

"Does she always speak in riddles?" Mum asked me.

"Way too often."

"Oh, you fools. You absolute *fools*." Natasha turned to look at us now, and her eyes flashed. "Do you not know who he is? Do you not know what you've brought here, to the worst possible place? *You*," she added to Joy, her voice absolutely livid, "I will deal with you later. For now, you need to get out before your daughter sees you and brings ruin down on *all* our heads."

My heart slammed into my ribs. "What did you just say?"

"His *daughter*," Pip whispered. "It can't be."

It couldn't be. It just couldn't. He was a ghost. He was our friend. He was Joy.

Joy.

A word I could easily have misheard over the sound of the crashing waves, a word that sounded so much like the name—

"Behold," said Natasha bitterly, pointing an accusing finger at the ghost who'd followed us for days. "King Jai."

24

The silence in the castle was somehow bigger and noisier than any sound. No one seemed able to speak.

"Well, I'll give you this much," Lej said to Joy at last, with a humorless laugh. "Looks like everything you touch *does* turn to ash and ruin."

Natasha had turned back to Joy. Her voice hissed through her teeth. "How are you here? I bespelled you."

"The spell broke when the gandaberunda set Kaveri loose," Joy (no, *Jai*) said, so quietly we could barely hear him. He was still looking at the floor. "I should have died of old age half a century ago, but your transformation made it impossible. I have become a ghost instead, unable to leave this world until I have put right what I did. Of course," he went on glumly, "I am not capable of putting anything right, so I will probably be like this forever."

"It is no more than you deserve," Natasha said. "She was your *child*."

"Yes," the ghost said heavily. "And my regret will not undo what I did, but know that I *have* regretted it."

It was impossible to look at Jai the same way now that I knew who he was. All the fondness I'd felt for him had soured. This was the king who could have stopped Sura's curse by giving back what his grandfather had stolen, and yet he'd chosen not to. This was the monster who had betrayed and condemned his own child just because he'd been afraid of losing the love of his kingdom.

"This is bad," said Pip. The gold binding ring, which hung around his neck like a collar, winked in the light. "This is really, *really* bad. We've come here with the two people in the world Kaveri has the most reason to hate. We don't stand a chance!"

"Maybe we should leave while we can," Jojo said uncertainly. "Maybe she doesn't yet know who we've got with us."

But the moment he said the words, I knew he was wrong.

Something trembled in the castle, something deep in the walls. Mum let out a startled gasp, and I turned to her at once, only to see that she was staring at the pink stone of the wall right beside her, where water had started to trickle from between the cracks in the stone.

"Run," I whispered. *"Run."*

It was too late. A girl stood in the doorway, but she wasn't like any other girl I'd ever seen. She was just water, silvery and furious and frothy, from her long hair to her torso to her toes, just water playacting at being a girl.

A blink later, the girl flung out a hand. Water shook loose from her, arcing across the air like a blade, and then it was around Jai, watery chains pinning him to the wall. The other hand shot out, another blade of water streaked across the room, and then Natasha was pinned against the opposite wall with the same watery chains around her.

"You left me to spend eternity in the dark," the girl said, turning her face from one to the other. Her voice was the same voice I'd heard when I'd gone to that lonely, dark place. It was the raw, broken voice of someone who hadn't been able to speak in a hundred years.

Neither Jai nor Natasha could reply, both their mouths covered by wet chains.

She would drown them like she'd almost drowned the Asura in the Magicwood, like she'd almost drowned Lej and me. I didn't know if she'd be able to kill a ghost, but she'd definitely be able to kill a witch.

"Stop!" I begged. "Don't do this, please!"

Water seethed across the floor and swished around my feet. The wheels of Jojo's chair sloshed and slipped. I understood the threat. If we tried to stop her, we'd drown, too.

The water was ice-cold, piercing through my shoes and socks and skin and getting all the way to my bones, but it didn't rise any higher. Out of the corner of my eye, I saw Pip flapping his wings to keep himself in the air. There was no way Kaveri would let him get close to her.

She tilted her head at me, curious. "What are you?" she said, the same question she'd asked me before. "You are not of this world, worldbuilder."

"Girl," I said, like before. "I'm a girl. And so are you."

"No, I am a creature of the shadows," she spat. "I am

more powerful than any girl. And I will see them punished for what they did to me."

Mum's eyes met mine, and I knew she was thinking the same thing I was. *People like us don't often get to feel powerful.*

"I think I understand why you want so badly to punish them," I said, taking another step closer. "Why you won't let them go, why it matters so much to you that you're powerful. It's because you're afraid of feeling like you did before. You're afraid of being powerless again."

"I will *never* be powerless again!"

"Kiki," Lej rasped. "I don't think Natasha has long."

Natasha's purple eyes were wide and panicked. She thrashed against the chains.

I shot a quick look at Pip. Understanding that I probably stood the best chance at getting close to Kaveri, that she was at least curious enough about me to not strike me down each time I took a step closer, he flapped a little lower.

"At least let Natasha go!" Suki pleaded. "She didn't know what your father was going to do. She'll drown if you don't let her go!"

In the fraction of the second that Kaveri's attention

was on Suki, Pip dipped his head and dropped the binding ring into my hand. I closed my fist around it quickly, feeling the curved edges where it would open, where I would have to clamp it around Kaveri's wrist.

"Let them drown," Kaveri said to Suki with reckless fury. "*I* have been drowning for a hundred years. Let them know what it feels like."

"Show me," I blurted out.

"Kiki."

That was Mum, but I couldn't turn back now. I took another step. "Show me what it was like for you," I said, holding out a hand, the hand without the binding ring in it. "Your father and Natasha and Sura have all told their stories, but you've never been allowed to tell yours. You can tell me now. Help me understand what they did to you."

Kaveri's silvery eyes were riveted on mine. "Why?" she asked coldly.

I thought fast. "Because I'm the worldbuilder," I said. "I can do things even you can't."

Like free you from the dark. I didn't say it out loud because I couldn't bring myself to lie outright to her, but

I knew it was what she'd be thinking. It was maybe the only thing that would let me get close.

As the sounds of Jai and Natasha thrashing grew quieter, Kaveri seemed to make up her mind. She reached for my outstretched hand with her own.

And I was gone.

Cold, empty shadows swept over me and erased what I was. I was no one. I was an abyss. I was darkness itself.

Tentatively, light blossomed into the darkness, and a story unfolded. There was a girl, even younger than I was, running barefoot and laughing across the grounds of Mysore Palace. As the girl grew, she was curious and kind. She loved the color pink, archery, and conch shells. She supported her father when his ministers demanded more than he could give. She explored her kingdom, searching for wrongs she could right. She laughed and laughed and *laughed.*

She had many friends, but one stood out: a witch with power humming at her fingertips and a smile on her face that looked like the stars coming out at night. They grew together, the girl and the witch, living golden day after golden day, until a curse ended it.

Abruptly, the light died and the story turned into shadows. Inside the shadows, a girl stood against a terrible, unseen force, holding back the tide. She laughed even then, hopeful and eager because she knew she had done everything in her power to save the kingdom and people she loved so much. But when the darkness didn't end and the shadows didn't lift, hope turned into something else. Disbelief, then heartbreak, and finally, rage.

Crushed by the tide of a curse that only she could hold back, and consumed with fury, the girl waited in the endless, lonely dark. And waited. And waited.

Her time would come.

And when it did, she would drown the world.

"Now you know," a voice said to me. "Now you see."

Just as quickly as I vanished, I was back. I blinked in the vivid golden light of the castle, in the here and now, and tears spilled down my cheeks.

Because *I* was back, but she wasn't. She was still in the dark. She had been released from the riverbed, but she had never left that terrible, cold, lonely place she'd been trapped in.

Kaveri had told me her story because I'd tricked her

into thinking I would help her. I could reach over right now and clasp the binding ring around her wrist. It would be so easy. And when that was done, she'd be powerless. The river would flow again. The Kikiverse would be safe. I would have saved it. I wouldn't have failed.

But what kind of person would I be if I did that? What kind of kingdom would I be saving if I saved it like that?

Only days ago, I'd still had this idea in my head that the Kikiverse had been a golden, perfect place before Mahishasura had cast his horned shadow over it. Now I knew that wasn't true. This universe was marvelous and surprising and it would always mean the world to me, but it had never been perfect.

And that was okay. It had been what I'd needed when I'd needed it most, but I was starting to be okay with the fact that it wasn't mine anymore.

But I still had the power to make a choice that would decide what kind of universe it would be tomorrow, and the day after, and the day after that, whether I was here or not.

I raised the hand that held the ring.

Clink.

It was the sound of the gold binding ring hitting the floor. I would not use it.

Kaveri's silver eyes dropped to the ring. I saw her recognize it and understand what I'd almost done. Her mouth opened in a cry of rage.

"Wait!" I cried.

Jagged blades of water exploded outward—

And froze.

My hands had automatically come up to shield my head. I lowered them in astonishment now, staring at the blade of water suspended in the air a scant inch in front of my face. There were dozens of other identical blades of water suspended around Kaveri and me, each of them striking out at me, at Mum, at the Crows.

Up on the walls, Jai, Natasha, and their watery chains had all gone completely still. Even Kaveri was frozen, her mouth open mid-cry.

No. Wait. They weren't *frozen*. The water, Jai, Natasha, and Kaveri were all still moving, but *so* slowly that it looked at first glance like they weren't moving at all.

So why was *I* still moving the same way I always had? I turned around and saw that the others were all looking at me and at one another with equally stunned expressions on their faces.

Except for Jojo. "It worked," he said, blinking like he couldn't believe his eyes. "It *worked*."

"*You* did this?" I asked incredulously.

He nodded. "I slowed time down. Those strands of hair I took from you, they were the thing I was missing. Everything's slowed down. We're not affected because we're all wearing the bracelets I made."

Mum abruptly sat down on the edge of the chariot. "Don't mind me," she said. "I'm just going to quietly freak out over here. Also," she added, pointing, "maybe someone should rescue those two."

Oh. Oops.

The twins, Lej, and I ran over to the ghost and witch pinned to the wall. Their chains were made out of water, so they were impossible to shift, but Jai and Natasha were not. Seizing them by the arms and legs, we dragged them free of the water and lowered them to the floor so that Suki could shove potions down their throats and revive them.

"They'll be okay, I think," she said, kneeling beside

them. "We got to them in time. It'll probably be something of a shock to them that one minute they were drowning and the next they're on the floor with a very bitter taste in their mouths, but they'll get over that."

"So you're telling me you knew you could slow time down," Lej said to Jojo in disbelief, "and you decided not to do it any sooner?"

"I thought Kiki would put the binding ring on Kaveri! I didn't think we'd need to slow time down!"

I almost flinched as six pairs of eyes landed on me.

"Did you *mean* to drop the binding ring?" Pip asked me.

I took a deep breath. "Yes. I couldn't do it. I *won't* do it. I don't know how long I was in the dark with her, but it was the coldest, loneliest, most horrible thing. And I *know* how it feels to be frightened and alone, but this was worse than anything I've ever felt before. I won't trap her there again."

Lej's jaw clenched. "Are you serious? We agreed that this was the only way."

"Well, I'm un-agreeing!" I shot back.

"You don't get to do that!" Lej shouted. "You don't get to just *decide* the fate of this universe while the rest of us get no say!"

I let out an incredulous laugh. "Are *you* serious? Isn't that why I'm here? Haven't you spent the past three days looking at me every time you didn't know what to do? Didn't you cross between universes and bring me here *because* Ashwini's gone and you needed someone else to make the difficult choices for you?"

Lej's face went white. Suki took a wobbly step back like my words had slammed her in the chest. "We didn't do that!" She looked at the others with something like panic. It was like Ashwini was right here with us, a phantom we all pretended we couldn't see. "We didn't, did we?"

I let out a shuddering breath and rubbed the back of my fist against my forehead, wondering if I'd gone too far. I tried to quiet the chaos inside my mind.

One thought tugged free of the mess, and I reached for it. It was the only thing that sounded right.

"This *isn't* something I get to decide alone," I said at last, "but what I do get to decide is what *I* do or don't do. I won't do this. If you want to, then one of you should pick up the binding ring and do it."

Power came and went, but it was like Mum said: no matter how much or how little I had, I would always be me.

It was the most difficult thing I'd done, but I let the

power go. This was not my world to save or destroy anymore. It was theirs.

"Do what you need to," I said quietly.

Pip, who was never short of an opinion, kept uncharacteristically silent. Unlike the others, he knew he had a lot less to lose and maybe he thought it wasn't up to him to decide, either.

As the most softhearted, Samara was the first to look away. Then Jojo did, too. Suki's chin trembled, and she held out for a while, but her eyes flicked to that look of betrayal frozen on Kaveri's face, and her shoulders dropped with a mixture of defeat and relief.

It was just Lej left. I knew he'd do it. He would hate it, but he would do it because he didn't think there was any other way.

"Okay." Mum, who had been very quiet for the past few minutes, stood up, brushed off her jeans, and put a gentle hand on Lej's shoulder. "This isn't easy, I know that, but I think it's obvious that no one here actually *wants* to imprison Kaveri. Jojo's given us all the gift of time, so why don't we use it to give ourselves a second to think and calm ourselves down? The hard choices can wait another minute."

I crossed my arms tightly, feeling like the worst kind of traitor. On the one hand, I knew it would be wrong to bind Kaveri, take away the only power she had, and force her to hold back Sura's curse again. On the other hand, the Crows had trusted me to save them and the rest of the Kikiverse, and I'd just pretty much told them I wasn't going to do that.

Why did letting them have the power to decide for themselves feel so much like abandoning them?

"There's an in-between, you know," Mum said softly to me, as if she'd seen my thoughts written all over my face. "There's a way to do the right thing *and* protect this world. You just need to find it."

"Me? Didn't we just have a conversation about how I don't get to pick a path for everyone?"

"I'm not asking you to pick a path for everyone, Kiki," she said. "I want you to find a new path altogether."

I stared at her. "As if it's that easy!"

"There's nothing easy about this," Mum said. "You and I both know it would have been easier to just bind Kaveri now and worry about everything else later, but you chose not to do that."

I felt my cheeks grow hot. "My brain has a bad habit of making things more difficult."

Mum snorted. "You decided not to take the easy way out because you're *kind*, and that's absolutely nothing to be ashamed of. Kiki, look at me," she said firmly when I fixed my eyes on the floor. "You have this way of talking about your brain like it's the worst part of you, but don't you see that it's one of the best?"

"I definitely don't see *that*," I said with a bit of a laugh. "I know what it's like, Mum. And I'm okay with it."

"I'd like for you to be more than *okay* with it," she replied, exasperated. "Haven't you noticed you never take the easy way out? Some of us are definitely born with great kindness in us, but I also think kindness is something we *choose*. You chose it when Ashwini asked you for your help and you gave it. You chose it when you decided not to break the gandaberunda's eye and eliminate this world, even though you believed at the time that it was the only way to defeat Mahishasura. You chose it today. It's a choice you've made over and over. And I believe you make that choice *because* of your brain, not in spite of it."

I blinked at her, startled. Was that true? *Because*, she'd

said. Not *in spite of*. Understanding that there was no monster in my mind had been such a big step for me that I had sort of rooted myself to that moment and hadn't left it. I'd stopped feeling ashamed, and I had asked for the help I needed, but I'd gone on thinking of my brain as something I needed to work *around*, not something that I could work *with*.

It was even in the way I thought about it. It was always *my brain* and *my mind*, as if I were constantly trying to put some distance between myself and it. As if it were a crooked tree growing in the middle of a path and forcing me to find a way around it, time and time again.

But that wasn't what it was. Yes, it got in my way sometimes, but it was also the thing that got me where I needed to go.

"You understand," Mum said, smiling at whatever she saw in my face.

"I'm who I am because of *all* of me," I said.

She rolled her eyes. "I think I may have mentioned that once or twice."

It was weird how obvious it seemed now, considering how long it had taken me to completely *get* it.

"And that's why it's you this universe needs right

now," Mum said. "The imagination that dreams up the hypothetical horrors that prey on you is the same imagination that created this extraordinary world. Your mind may be chaos, but it is also creativity, Kiki. Don't just be *okay* with that." She kissed me on top of my head. "It was your mind that dreamed up a way to defeat Mahishasura, remember? And it's your mind that will dream up a way to save this kingdom."

"For what it's worth, that is A-plus wisdom," Pip piped up, making me jump because I'd almost forgotten we weren't alone in the castle. "We could do worse than letting Mum make all our decisions for us."

"Is *everyone* calling me Mum now?" Mum wanted to know.

"Um, Kiki?" Jojo cleared his throat, his eyes on the slow progress of the jagged blades of water exploding out of Kaveri. "Just so you know, we don't have a whole lot of time left before the power in the bracelets runs out."

I wasn't paying attention. Something had snagged in my thoughts, and I went back to find it. It was the bit about how I'd once felt like there was a monster in my mind, but I'd been wrong.

I turned that thought over. Like a shiny pebble on the beach, I held it up to the light to get a better look at it.

After everything I'd discovered over the past few days, I had been so sure that there were a lot of monsters in this story, but maybe the truth was that there were none. Each one had done something monstrous, but that didn't make them monsters. Hadn't *I* done something monstrous when I'd conjured up a group of rebel orphans, a choice that had filled Ashwini with so much anger and resentment that *she'd* done something monstrous just to be free of the burden of looking after them?

It had been simpler with Mahishasura because he had chosen to be cruel and violent and had never tried to be anything else. King Mahindra, who'd had no horns and no antlers, had chosen to be a monster, too. But the other characters in this story weren't like that. Sura, Kaveri, and Jai had all made good *and* bad choices. They'd been kind *and* cruel *and* brave *and* cowardly. They'd tried to offer friendship. They'd tried to save their people. They'd tried to protect themselves. They'd all hurt other people when it went wrong. It was complicated.

And I couldn't help feeling like maybe that was the

answer I was looking for. From the start, I'd been thinking about this the same way I'd thought of Mahishasura, but maybe that was where I'd made a mistake. I'd been trying to defeat the monsters, but maybe what I really needed to do was *save* them.

All of them.

25

There was a way. I just had to find it.

It was like throwing out a half-finished painting and starting over. It wasn't easy, but it was what needed to be done. I had to ignore everything I knew, or thought I knew, and rethink everything. I had to go back to the empty canvas.

Back to the very beginning of the quest, to that moment when the gandaberunda showed me a vision.

A shadow with slender shoulders and long, spiky antlers. A ruby crown. The clasped hands of a king and a witch. Beasts so cold and crystalline they turned the air to frost with their breath. An urn tipping over. A girl alone in the—

I gasped so loudly, the others jumped.

"Ha!" Pip cried. "That's your light bulb face!"

"We can break the curse!"

Mum gave me a very Mum-ish "I told you so" look, but Lej clenched his hands into fists. I could tell he was afraid to get his hopes up. "How?"

"The only way. Sura's going to take it back."

"Why would she do that?"

"Because," I said, "we're going to give her the one thing she wants."

I told them. I explained where we'd gone wrong and what I'd just figured out, and how the gandaberunda had given us the answers at the very beginning, and how we needed *all* of the pieces of the puzzle to make this work. Then we decided how we were going to do it.

Together.

I picked up the gold binding ring.

When time went back to normal, Kaveri was so startled that the blades of water wobbled in the air and fell to the floor with a splash. Only an instant had passed for her, but somehow I wasn't right in front of her anymore, and somehow Natasha and Jai were coughing and rising from the floor.

"What"—bewildered, the Good Witch spat out a mouthful of water—"what did you do to me?"

"The words you're looking for are 'thank you,'" Pip chirped.

I held the binding ring up so Kaveri could see it, knowing we had only seconds to make her understand before she drowned us all in her rage.

"Look," I said. And I snapped the binding ring in two. "It's not a trick, I promise. No one's going to bind you."

She eyed the two halves of the ring, that look of betrayal still on her face. "You were going to."

"I know, and I'm sorry." I dropped the pieces to the floor. "It's over."

Her eyes met mine. They were silver and cold and full of suspicion. "You expect me to believe you'll sacrifice the kingdom to the curse instead?"

"No, we're going to save the kingdom," I said, and turned to Jai. "That part is up to you, Jai."

Jai, who stood a little way away from us, his blurry shoulders hunched and dejected, looked up in bewilderment.

"This is how you put things right," I said. I held out a hand. "Give me your crown."

He blinked. "My crown?"

"Your ruby crown," I said. "Everyone thinks the crown was a myth, but I know it wasn't. You had it when you were transformed into a tree. That's why you were the last king to be seen with it. And when the spell broke, you must have still had it."

"I hid it," said Jai, still confused. "I didn't want anyone to know I was a king."

Suki poked him in the ribs. "Get the crown, then," she said. "We don't have all day."

Jai blinked some more. "Well, I suppose there's no reason why you can't have it," he said dubiously, and just like that, the crown was in my hand, probably summoned from the same in-between place he vanished to from time to time. "I'm afraid I don't see how that will put anything right, but if you want it so badly, who am I to argue?"

I clutched the crown, my breath catching. "The reason you don't understand," I said, my voice trembling as I held out my other hand for Lej's knife, "is because the one thing you did right was tell Sura the truth when she asked you to return her heart. You *didn't* know anything about it."

I used the knife to pry the large, shining ruby out of the heart of the crown.

The one with a crack down the middle.

I tossed the crown back to Jai and held the large ruby up. “You didn’t know King Mahindra had hidden Sura’s heart in plain sight.”

Kaveri’s eyes were riveted to the ruby. Natasha’s mouth fell open. It was quite possibly the most satisfying thing I’d seen in a while. She touched a tentative finger to the ruby, and it pulsed faintly with life. She looked up at me. “How did you know?”

“When I went back to the start to rethink everything, I realized we went wrong when we assumed the ruby crown was just a clue pointing us to King Jai,” I explained. “Once I worked that out, I put it all together. The crown was first seen during King Mahindra’s reign and last seen during King Jai’s. It had a cracked ruby in the middle. Sura’s heart was broken. It all added up.”

“You can break the curse for good?” Kaveri’s voice wasn’t quite steady, and there was an echo in it of the selfless girl she had once been. “And free me?”

“Yep,” Pip said merrily.

Natasha objected. “We *can’t* free her without the—”

"The urn?" I interrupted. "The one Jai broke? Ever since we met him, he's been talking about putting something right. And he can't have been talking about Sura's heart, because he didn't know he had it. The only thing he *could* have been talking about was the thing he *actually* did wrong. The broken urn."

"I kept it," Jai blurted out. "I kept the pieces. You cursed me before I could tell you. And when the gandaberunda freed me, I kept coming to your lighthouse to tell you then, and each time I lost my nerve."

"Can you fix it?" Kaveri whispered, her eyes on Natasha.

"No," said Natasha, but a smile played at the corners of her mouth. She pointed at me. "But *she* can."

"The problem is, I don't know where it is," Jai admitted in the resigned voice of someone who thinks they're doomed to keep getting things wrong. "I kept the pieces safe with my most prized possessions, but I don't know what became of them when I was cursed and my reign ended."

"*We* know where it is," I said. "The pieces of the urn are in the same place all the possessions of past kings go. In fact, *you* walked right past it," I said to Natasha, grinning at the stupefied look on her face. "We were all so busy with Sura's antler, we didn't pay any attention to the broken vases in the Restricted and Highly Unsafe section of the Ancient Library."

"You—I—" Natasha was at a loss for words.

"Less talking, more teleportation," Pip said to her. "Once we've got the urn, you can break the spell on Kaveri, and then we—"

"No!" Kaveri said quickly. "Break Sura's curse first. I can wait. The people who need water can't."

I nodded and turned to Natasha. "Then maybe you could get us all to the Void?"

With a wave of Natasha's hand, we were all engulfed in a bubble of light, and we left the castle behind. An instant later, we stood in the shadows of the bridge over the Void, dizzy and disoriented from Natasha's spell, and the Magicwood was ahead of us.

"Gah," Mum choked out, looking a bit green.

Something glowed in the shadows. I took a step closer to it, waiting for it to come to me.

It was a cold, crystalline cat-creature, baring its teeth. "You are either very brave or very foolish to come back here, worldbuilder," it snarled in Sura's voice.

I held up the shining ruby in my hand. "I think this is yours."

"A stone?"

"That's just an illusion. Look closer."

I saw the moment she recognized it. The cat-creature's face transformed, and something like a strangled howl came out of its mouth.

"Show the Good Witch how to find you, and let her bring you here," I said. "And if you take your curse back, I'll mend your heart and give it back to you."

"All the pieces of the puzzle," Mum said quietly.

I nodded. "Everything the gandaberunda showed me was tied together, connected. It didn't just let Kaveri out of the riverbed. It broke the spell on Jai, too, because it knew we needed him." I looked from Natasha to Kaveri to Jai to the cat-creature, all shocked and silent. "We need to make things right for *all* of you. That's the only way to save the kingdom."

Sura let out a sound that might have been a sob. "Come get me, witch."

"I do not like your tone," Natasha said haughtily, but she wanted this as much as anyone, so she laid a hand on the cat-creature's back, and they both winked out of existence.

When she returned moments later, a weak and paper-thin Sura beside her, I took my pencil out and drew a line down the middle of the ruby. It mended itself, the illusion around it shattering, and it transformed in my hand into something red, beating, and alive.

That was, after all, the best thing about the power I held in my pencil. It could conjure armies made from tin and bring a whole palace down on a demon king's head, but it could also put broken things back together.

I handed the mended heart to Sura, who let out another sob as she cradled it in her hands. As it beat in her palm, I watched as her shoulders straightened, her faded fur flooded with new color, and her antlers gleamed white. With a soft, relieved breath, Sura pushed her heart into her chest.

There was a silent rip in the air, like something unseen had rippled across the entire Kikiverse. The shadows over the Void lifted.

Sura bowed her antlered head. "It is done, world-builder."

"Are you going?" I asked.

"I am," she said. "I will rest at last."

And, finally able to die, her eyes filled with light. Slowly, gently, like a tree shedding its leaves, she dissolved into dust.

We watched as it drifted away on the wind.

"Is"—Lej's voice cracked—"is the curse broken?"

Behind me, Samara gasped. "Look!"

As the shadows of the Void lifted completely, we saw dozens upon dozens of Sura's glowing, crystalline beasts come out of the Magicwood. They were running, wild and joyous and mesmerizing, and the moment they leaped into the dry, rocky riverbed, they weren't beasts anymore.

They were water.

"When Sura cursed the kingdom, the water of the stolen river had to go somewhere," I reasoned. "I think she created an army of ice beasts out of it. And now they're home."

Stunned and awed, we watched as the river came back.

"Ahem," said Natasha. "Which of you will undertake the thankless task of persuading Numa to part with the pieces of the urn?"

"*You* will," I said firmly. "You and Jai are the ones who need to put this part right."

"I think," Natasha said after a moment, "that perhaps I'll steal it."

Before anyone could protest, she blinked out of existence and blinked right back again, holding three pieces of pottery in her arms.

Samara looked distressed. "Numa will never let me set foot in the library if he finds out I helped *steal* from it!"

"That child has some very peculiar priorities," Natasha informed the rest of us, her nose in the air.

Ignoring that, I took the pieces of the urn from her and laid them out on the bridge. I matched up the right edges like a jigsaw. Then I used my pencil to draw new seams and fused the pieces back together.

At last, the urn was whole.

I looked around for Kaveri, who had gone to the edge of the bridge to look into the river, the place she had been imprisoned for so long. Jai, almost completely faded, stood a few steps behind her. Neither of them said a word.

"Kaveri?" Natasha said tentatively. "I can break the spell I cast over you now. If you want me to."

Kaveri turned. She was almost golden in the sunset,

the light making rainbows out of the water of her hair, and she trembled.

Somewhere in the dark, the girl was afraid. She'd forgotten how to live in the light.

But she'd once been as brave as she'd been kind, so she took Natasha's outstretched hand.

In a tremendous flash of white light, Kaveri was gone. I caught a glimpse of the urn, rising into the air and hovering in the light, and then the urn was gone, too. The light scattered into rainbows across the bridge before fading at last, leaving behind a girl with long dark hair and unsure brown eyes.

Jai started to cry. Then Natasha started to cry. Then Kaveri started to cry.

"Aw," Suki said joyfully, clasping her hands to her heart.

"Right," said Mum, taking me by the arm and herding the Crows down the bridge back in the direction of the city. "This is the part where we let them have a moment alone. I think they've earned it after a hundred years, don't you?"

26

"Funny how simple that was in the end, don't you think?" Suki said, her mouth full of stew.

Exhausted and overwhelmed, not one of us bothered to dignify that with a reply.

Not that Simha would have spoken even if he'd had something to say. He was sulking on the other side of the kitchen, deeply offended that we hadn't waited for him to come back from the trial before racing off to finish our quest, and he had already promised us that it would be *years* before he would forgive us.

Jai was gone. He'd come to say goodbye, and then, like Sura, he had been set free. I didn't know what he and Kaveri had said to each other, but whatever it was, it must have been enough to make him feel like it was his time to go. As for Kaveri, she would live at the lighthouse with Natasha. The Good Witch seemed to think that, given time, she would recover and remember how to be human, and maybe even take her place as the ruler of the kingdom one day.

Chamundeshwari would *love* that.

Time was what I needed, too. I was still learning so much about myself and my place in both universes.

Perched on my shoulder, Pip's quick beak darted out and pecked a piece of Mysore pak right out of my hand. With a merry, unrepentant laugh, he flew away before I could snatch it back.

He was still here, and he'd said he wasn't going anywhere yet. Maybe he was still afraid of whatever came next. Maybe he, the Crows, and I had more quests and adventures ahead of us. Maybe his unfinished business wasn't finished yet. It was a lot of maybes, and I'd once struggled with so much uncertainty, but I was beginning to see that the hope and possibilities hiding inside all those maybes were actually pretty great.

"So, I didn't want to say anything before," Suki said, her voice unusually tentative, "but I saw something weird when our first chariot crashed and we were fighting off the beasts in the Magicwood. There was someone else there with us. They saved me from one of the beasts, and they got Kiki out of the wreck of the chariot. It all happened so fast and there was so much going on that I'd just assumed I'd gotten confused and it was actually one of you, but the more I think about it, the more I'm sure."

"Sure of what?" Jojo asked her.

"That it was Ashwini."

I looked at her, startled.

"That's not possible," Lej said quietly. "I know you want to believe she's still close by and watching our backs, but she isn't. How could she have known we were there, anyway? We were deep in the Magicwood, deeper than any of us had ever gone before."

"It was her," said Suki stubbornly. "I know it was."

I stood up abruptly and was out the door so fast that even Mum didn't have time to ask questions.

My mind spun as I raced past the Kiki statue, across the square, and followed the busy streets back to Sentinel's Tower. But I didn't go to see the gandaberunda. Instead, I stood outside the graffitied walls and searched the artwork until I found what I was looking for.

Hidden amid the rest of the graffiti was a curling, looping line painted in rainbow colors. It looked like it was just there for decoration, but I knew what it really was. A rainbow thread, like the thread I'd pulled off my pajamas and tied around the bottom of a hiding staircase.

I'd put it there so that Ashwini and I, who had been trying to get to the top of the palace, would be able to tell the two hiding staircases apart. It was a small thing in a story filled with far more exciting things. I'd almost forgotten about it.

And I was pretty sure that I'd never mentioned it to anyone else.

I traced the painted thread with my finger and waited.

It didn't take long. It felt like it was just a few minutes before a familiar shadow fell against the wall beside me.

"You painted the thread," I said.

"You wouldn't be here if you didn't know that already," said the shadow in Ashwini's voice.

"You were in the Magicwood when we crashed." I took a step away from the wall. "And it was you who pulled Lej and me out of Lake Lune when we almost drowned, wasn't it? We thought it was Jai, but it couldn't have been. He was afraid of the water."

The shadow shrugged.

I turned to look at her, the first of the Crows, the fierce, brave warrior girl I'd created and broken. Her hair was almost to her shoulders now, and her nose was freckled by the sun, but the firm, stubborn chin and red leather jacket were exactly as I remembered them.

"I thought I'd dreamed you in the forest," I said. There was a lump in my throat, and I didn't know what else to say. I couldn't look at her without thinking of the way she'd betrayed us, but I also couldn't look at her without thinking of the fierce, funny friend she'd been to me for a little while. "Where have you been?"

"Around," she said. Something flickered in her face. "Pip came back, didn't he? As a crow? I saw him, but I almost didn't believe it."

I nodded. "Here," I said, tugging my bracelet off and holding it out to her. "I'm not going to need protection from spells and curses in London. And if you're going to keep looking out for the Crows, you never know when you might need to slow time down."

Surprised, she took the bracelet. As she pushed the sleeve of her jacket up to put it on her wrist, something on her skin caught the light.

I froze.

Because there were looping gold letters tattooed around Ashwini's wrist. *S*, then another *S*. Then *J*. Then *L*. And finally, *K*.

The twins, Jojo, Lej, and me.

My eyes darted away from the tattooed letters and landed on the tattoo on my wrist. And it occurred to me all of a sudden that maybe the shape that the three small gold lines made wasn't supposed to be a triangle, after all.

Maybe it was supposed to be the letter *A*.

"*You* put these tattoos on us," I said, stunned.

She winced, instinctively putting a hand over her own tattoo to hide it, but it was too late for that. "They're runes, not tattoos," she admitted. "Each one is keyed to the rune I put on each of you."

"But why?" I asked, and then I realized I already knew. "They tell you when we're in trouble, don't they? That's how you were able to get to Lej and me in time to pull us out of the lake. That's how you found us in the Magicwood."

She didn't answer, but she didn't have to.

"That's a lot of trouble to go to."

She didn't reply to that, either. My heart ached. Even after everything she had done to be free of the terrible burden and responsibility of keeping herself and the other Crows safe, she hadn't been able to bring herself to abandon them. To abandon *us*.

"How were you able to get to us so fast?"

She smiled faintly, a ghost of the merry, reckless grin that had once lit her face up. "You're not the only one with friends in the Witches' Guild."

I let myself smile back, just a little.

"Time to go," she said. "Don't tell the others you saw me."

"Are you *ever* going to go back to Crow House?"

She turned to walk away. "See you around, Kiki" was all she said. "Try to stay out of trouble."

So I went back to Crow House with a mostly convincing story about how I'd needed to talk to the gandaberunda. I wasn't sure Pip believed me, and for all I knew he'd followed me and had been one of the crows I'd seen in the sky, but the others didn't ask any questions.

Natasha was in the house, waiting for me. "Here," she said without ceremony, handing me a ring made out of twisted strands of silver. "Pointer finger, not any of the others. And you," she said to Pip, putting a smaller ring around one of his skinny crow ankles. "You're welcome."

"Um, what *is* it?" he demanded.

"The tear will close shortly after you go back to London," she said. "Those rings will allow you to freely cross between universes."

I blinked down at the ring. "That sounds like *really* powerful magic."

"I do not know if you've noticed," said Natasha, "but I am *really* powerful. Also, you are the worldbuilder."

"So what you're saying," said Pip, "is that it's Kiki's power that makes it possible just as much as yours."

I poked him. "Shut it, or she'll take the rings back."

"Now I must go," Natasha said, sweeping imperiously out of the room. "Simha, come to the lighthouse for tea this afternoon. We have to talk about Numa."

Simha perked up. "What has that ghastly gargoyle done now?"

"You wouldn't believe me if I told you! But it's not for innocent ears," she added primly when Pip and I both looked interested in knowing what Numa had done this time.

Mum stuck her head in the room to say: "When grown-ups say that, they usually mean they want a good old-fashioned gossip."

"Well, I do, and I'm not ashamed of it," said Natasha, and left.

Once she'd gone, Pip and Suki tried to convince Mum to make them a second lunch. I left them to it. There was one more thing I had to do before I left the Kikiverse.

I owed a very nice fisherman a new boat.

Once I'd sketched a few lines and constructed the right shape out of a piece of wood, I took it outside, and Samara cast the spell to make it full-size. We could have given it to the fisherman as it was, but I thought the plain wooden planks were crying out for a cheerful coat of paint. So Mum and I worked on it side by side, and then the others came out and helped, too, until the boat was a riotous hodgepodge of color.

"Mum?" I said, stepping back to admire the boat. "When we go home, could we maybe look at your old sketchbook at some point? The one with the world *you* created? You said Dad loved it," I explained when she looked at me in surprise. "And you must have, too, right? So I think it'd be nice to see it."

She rubbed at a smear of paint on her cheek, a small smile on her face. "That sketchbook is a piece of some of the happiest *and* the most painful parts of my life. I don't think I'm ready to face it yet, but I'll get it out for you. There's no reason why *you* can't look at it."

It was funny, but I could have said almost exactly the same thing about *my* sunshine-yellow sketchbook. It was a piece of *me*, from a time that had been both incredibly difficult and full of so much joy. Chaos and creativity. That was what Mum had said up in my castle in the sky. My brain overflowed with both, and that sometimes made things very difficult, but it was also . . . *fun*.

I was kind of excited to see what I'd come up with next.

Mum watched me suspiciously. "I hope you're planning to stay put for the time being," she said. "Try not to jump into *my* world next time."

I laughed. "I'm not making any promises."

FIND OUT HOW IT ALL BEGAN!

Kiki is shocked to discover that she has drawn a whole imaginary world into existence. But does she have the power to erase its most wicked villain before he destroys everything?

ACKNOWLEDGMENTS

When I first sat down to write this book, *Kiki Kallira Breaks a Kingdom* hadn't published yet. It wasn't my first book, but it was the one closest to my heart, and I had no idea how readers would react to my creative, anxious heroine and her weird, wonderful world. The funny thing about acknowledgments, though, is that authors write them much later, often after the book is written and edited. So as I write these particular words, Kiki's first adventure *has* made its way into the world, and I've had the incredible experience of hearing from young readers in the months since.

Which is why that's where I want to start, with an

enormous thank-you to the readers who have followed Kiki all this way. Your support, excitement, and enthusiastic messages have made a difficult 2021 a thousand times brighter.

A few other incredibly important thank-yous:

To my husband, who makes it possible for me to write these stories.

To my children, who make me laugh.

To my parents, who gave me my first stories.

To my agent, Penny Moore, who this book is dedicated to. You've helped me make so many of my author dreams come true and have always, unfailingly, been a light guiding me through the woods. I'm so proud to call you my friend.

To my editor, Jenny Bak, who listens patiently to my messy ideas and helps me transform them into a much, much better book. Thank you for fighting for Kiki and me.

To the rest of the wonderful team at Viking and Penguin Random House, who have gone to bat for Kiki: Gaby Corzo, Kate Frentzel, Delia Davis, and Vivian Kirklin, for the patience and diligence that went into editing, copyediting, and rereading the manuscript; Vanessa Robles,

Kelley Brady, and Kate Renner, for the design and production that turned that manuscript into this actual book; Nabi H. Ali, for yet another gorgeous cover illustration; and Kim Ryan, Kaitlin Kneafsey, Alex Garber, Lauren Festa, Brianna Lockhart, Christina Colangelo, Summer Ogata, and countless others, for the tireless work that has gone into the subrights, publicity, marketing, and promotion of Kiki's story.

To every bookstore, book buyer, librarian, and teacher who has so fiercely championed Kiki's story over the past year. I can't thank you enough.

To Jamie, for being such a fantastic early reader.

And finally, to my author peers, who inspire me every single day. It is a privilege to create stories alongside you.

Love,

Sangu